Meet the Fortunes—three generations of a family with a legacy of wealth, influence and power. As they gather for a host of weddings, passionate new romances are ignited…and shocking family secrets are revealed…

CHLOE FORTUNE: The young debutante thought she'd outwitted her overly protective, matchmaking relatives by getting engaged to her brother's best friend. Only problem—she fell in love with her pretend groom. Chloe's all set to end the masquerade, but it looks like the groom's been keeping his own secrets!

MASON CHANDLER: This powerful MD wants to settle down with the only woman he's ever loved. But suddenly his double life catches up with him, threatening his one chance at happiness…

KATE FORTUNE: This family matriarch suspects that Chloe and Ma̶ of the Fortune fam

Fortune Family Tree

Caleb Fortune * m. Lilah Dulaine

Stuart Fortune m. Marie Smith

[2] GARRETT Fortune
--m.--
Renee Riley

[3] JACK Fortune
--1st m.--
Sandra Alexander (d)
--b--
Lily Fortune

--2nd m.--
Amanda Corbain

[4] MOLLIE SHAW **
--m.--
Gray McGuire

Emmet Fortune m. Annie Mackenzie (d)

[1] MACKENZIE Fortune
--m.--
Kelly Sinclair

Chad Fortune
{

CHLOE Fortune
--m.--
Mason Chandler

Key:
[1] The Honour-Bound Groom
[2] Society Bride
[3] The Secretary and the Millionaire
[4] The Groom's Revenge
[5] Undercover Groom

Symbols:
- - - - - Affair
{ Twins
* Kate Fortune's brother-in-law
** Child of Affair

Fortune's Children™

BRIDES

UNDERCOVER GROOM
Merline Lovelace

™SILHOUETTE®

*First published in Great Britain 2000
Silhouette Books, Eton House, 18-24 Paradise Road,
Richmond, Surrey TW9 1SR*

© Harlequin Books S.A. 1999

Special thanks and acknowledgement to
Merline Lovelace for her contribution to the
FORTUNE'S CHILDREN: THE BRIDES series.

ISBN 0 373 76220 8

26-0006

*Printed and bound in Spain
by Litografia Rosés S.A., Barcelona*

This is for Mary and Inga and Paula and Audrey and all the other wonderful readers who enjoy romances as much as I do. Thanks for your letters, your friendship and your words of encouragement!

MERLINE LOVELACE

spent twenty-three exciting years as an air force officer, serving tours at the Pentagon and at bases all over the world, before she began a new career as a novelist. When she's not tied to her keyboard, she and her own handsome hero, Al, enjoy travelling, golf and long, lively dinners with friends and family.

Merline enjoys hearing from readers, and can be reached at P.O. Box 892717, Oklahoma City, OK, 73189, USA.

Silhouette® is proud to present

Fortune's Children
B R I D E S

**Meet the Fortune brides: special women
who perpetuate a family legacy greater
than mere riches!**

April 2000
A FORTUNE'S CHILDREN WEDDING:
THE HOODWINKED BRIDE
Barbara Boswell

THE HONOUR-BOUND GROOM
Jennifer Greene

May 2000
SOCIETY BRIDE
Elizabeth Bevarly

THE SECRETARY AND THE MILLIONAIRE
Leanne Banks

June 2000
THE GROOM'S REVENGE
Susan Crosby

UNDERCOVER GROOM
Merline Lovelace

**Remember, where there's a bride…
there's a *wedding*!**

One

"**W**ait, Miss Fortune. I'll announce you."

Chloe Fortune aimed a smile over her shoulder at the trim, gray-haired executive assistant who hurried out of the copy center, her arms laden with a stack of documents.

"Never mind, Amy. I called Mr. Chandler earlier and told him I'd drop by sometime this afternoon."

"But he's got someone in his office...."

The older woman's protest trailed off as Chloe waved a crimson-tipped hand and sailed through the elegantly furnished reception area. Chloe had made enough visits to her fiancé's twentieth-floor office suite to know she always had immediate access.

A dazzling view of the Minneapolis skyline

drenched in late September sunshine filled the floor-to-ceiling windows on her right. Chloe didn't allow the spectacular view to distract her; it had taken her most of the morning to work up the courage for this visit. She had to do it now, before she lost her nerve.

This time she wouldn't wimp out.

This time she'd wait until Mason Chandler got rid of his visitor, then she'd either sweep everything off his burled mahogany desk and make wild, uninhibited love to him on its polished surface or— She gulped. Or she'd hand him back the four-carat emerald-cut solitaire he'd slipped on her ring finger last January.

Last January! She paused with her hand on the brass door latch, thinking of her unconventional engagement. She couldn't quite believe that she and Mase had been engaged for almost nine months. Or that they'd shared only a few casual kisses in all that time.

Okay, so maybe their self-imposed restraint had been part of the ground rules she'd laid down when she proposed to Mase. After all, she was the one who'd come up with the idea of a phony engagement in the first place. At the time it had seemed like the perfect answer to her dilemma.

She'd just returned to Minneapolis after two years in Paris, bringing home with her a degree in art history, a slightly bruised heart and a seriously dented ego. The degree she'd earned from the Paris Institute of Art. The damaged heart and ego she owed to handsome tennis star, Andre Couvier, who, she'd discovered, had loved the prospect of getting his hands on a chunk of her father's millions far more than he'd loved her. The last thing Chloe wanted when she got back to the States was to rush into another disastrous romance.

Unfortunately, she hadn't been able to convince her overly solicitous father that she was more interested in translating her degree into a viable marketing tool than in socializing. Emmet Fortune had exerted the kind of constant, loving pressure that only a father can, urging her to cut back on her long hours at the Fortune Corporation headquarters, to go out more, to enjoy her youth.

So-o-o-o...in desperation, Chloe had proposed to Mase.

The deal was simple. He would run cover for her with her father. In return, she'd take over the marketing campaign for Chandler Industries' latest twin-engine jet prototype. Since the VP for Marketing had just been caught with his hand in Mase's executive till, Chloe's offer had been deliberate, calculated and timely. Once he'd recovered from his initial surprise, Mase had agreed to her scheme readily enough.

She'd been sure he would. She'd known Mase Chandler off and on for most of her life—first as her older brother Mac's friend and then as an occasional escort. Unlike her fiercely overprotective father and older brother, however, Mase didn't take her personal ambitions lightly. Nor had he ever patronized her. He understood her need to prove she was as capable as any of her Fortune cousins. So she'd worked up the marketing campaign, and he'd agreed to act as her fiancé.

Their phony engagement had worked perfectly…at first. The match had certainly thrilled her father, who liked and respected Mase. It also allowed Chloe to devote every ounce of energy to learning the intricacies of the marketing and advertising worlds from the ground up. And Mase made the perfect fiancé. Easy, undemanding, relaxing to be with. Whenever he wasn't jetting off on one of his extended business trips, he and Chloe enjoyed each other's company at dinner and the theater.

She wasn't quite sure when or how the engagement had taken on a life of its own. She hadn't expected the diamond Mase slid onto her finger the night they announced their engagement to his family. Nor had she planned on giving in to her father's pressure to set a wedding date. That had sort of…happened. Before she knew it, she'd been roped into discussing gowns and menus and flowers with Mollie Shaw McGuire, the wedding planner who'd become such a close friend of the Fortune family.

Even worse, the pretend bride had somehow fallen hopelessly in love with her phony groom.

Looking back, Chloe couldn't pinpoint the exact moment it happened, couldn't pick a morning when she suddenly woke up and realized that she wanted her *fake* engagement to end in a *real* wedding. She only knew that she missed Mase when he was gone. That the hand he planted in the small of her back to guide her to a table burned right through whatever she was wearing. That she ached to peel off his hand-tailored suit, unknot his tie, unbutton his shirt and plant hot, greedy kisses all over his naked chest.

All of which she fully intended to do today.

If she didn't lose her nerve!

They couldn't continue the deception any longer. Mollie wanted to send the wedding invitations to the printers. Her father was already talking about endowing a chair at his alma mater to ensure his grandchildren got a quality education. Chloe either had to call the engagement off…or convince Mase to toss out their original ground rules and make wild, reckless love to her.

He wanted to. For all his deliberate restraint, Chloe sensed the desire he so carefully kept in check. She'd tried to hint that she was ready—more than ready!—for him to unleash it. This time, she vowed, she'd do more than just hint.

Dragging in a deep, steadying breath, Chloe pushed down the brass latch. The heavy oak door slid open noiselessly. She'd taken only a single step when the sound of a husky contralto floated across the luxurious office suite.

"Come on, Mase. You love what we do together. Surely you're not going to give it up just because you're engaged?"

The intimacy in the dark-as-chocolate voice brought Chloe up short. That…and the sight of a stunning brunette nestled comfortably between her fiancé's thighs.

Mase was leaning against the front edge of his desk. Beneath his neat black hair, his tanned face wore a smile that ripped at Chloe's heart. His hands rested on the brunette's waist, while hers played with his tie. The same silk tie that Chloe had envisioned slowly unknotting just seconds ago!

Her fingers balled into fists. She struggled for breath as a wave of raw emotion crashed over her and Mase replied in his rich, easy baritone, "No, I'm not giving it up because I'm engaged. I told you my reasons."

"None of which will matter when the fireworks start," his companion purred, tickling the underside of his jaw with the tie ends. "You're hooked, just like I am. You crave the thrill, the excitement, of our little games."

His smile tipped into a wry grin. "I don't think you can call what we do a game, Pam. We've taken it too close to the edge too many times."

"And that's what makes it so wonderful. What makes us so damned good together. You don't want to give it up, Mase. You know you don't. Besides, I need you. No one plays it harder or faster or rougher than you do."

Chloe choked. She didn't want to hear any more. She certainly didn't need to see any more. Now she

understood why Mase hadn't taken her up on her
subtle hints about morphing their pretend relationship into a real one. Only a fool would want to tie
himself to idiotic, naive Chloe, who had traveled all
the way to Paris to lose her virginity at the ripe old
age of twenty-four, when he could play hard and
fast and rough with this…this person.

Misery and a fury she had no right to feel coursed
through her. She must have made some movement,
some sudden jerk, because the brunette flicked a
quick look over Mase's shoulder.

Her brown eyes locked on the woman frozen in
the door, then filled with an expression that hovered
between recognition, amusement and—damn her!—
triumph. The message was immediate, unmistakable,
woman to woman.

*He's mine. He put an engagement ring on your
finger, lady, but we both know he's mine.*

Chloe's nails dug into her palms. Her chin shot
up at the exact moment Mase twisted around and
spotted her.

Another man might have stammered or flushed
with embarrassment at being caught in such intimacy by his supposed fiancée. Not Mase. Not calm,
controlled, always-in-command Mase.

"I'm sorry, Chloe. I didn't know you were here."

"Obviously not."

Unruffled, he moved his visitor to one side and
straightened. "Please, come in. I'd like you to meet
Pam Hawkins. She's a business associate of mine."

He didn't blush. Didn't even blink. Chloe had to admire his aplomb, even as she fought the hurt and fury tearing through her. She had no right to feel this awful jealousy, she reminded herself fiercely. Mase hadn't made her any promises. He'd helped her out when she asked him to, that's all. He was a friend. Only a friend.

The realization made her even more miserable. To compensate, she hiked her chin up another notch.

"I'm sorry I disturbed you."

"You didn't." He strolled over to usher her into the office, as cool as she was flushed. "We've finished our business."

His hand went to the small of her back in a touch so natural, so casually polite that Chloe's teeth ground together. Involuntarily she jerked away from his hand.

"You're finished?" she echoed. "Strange. From where I'm standing, it looked as though you were just getting started."

The tinge of red that crept into his cheeks gave her some satisfaction. Not much, but some.

"I'll talk to you another time," she said icily. "When you're not quite so busy."

With a regal nod to the brunette, she spun around and retraced her steps through the anteroom.

Mase caught up to her as she jabbed at the elevator button, blinking furiously to clear her eyes of a ridiculous sting of tears.

"I'm sorry you walked in on that. It's not what

it looks like—'' He broke off, his mouth twisting in disgust. ''I can't believe I just said that.''

Chloe couldn't, either. She started to point out acidly that every man ever caught cheating on his wife or girlfriend used the same, hackneyed line, but caught herself just in time. She wasn't Mase's girlfriend. Not really. And she certainly wasn't his wife.

''You don't have to explain anything. Not anymore. Not that you ever did.'' She stabbed the button again, trying for a coherency that eluded her. ''Oh, hell, I'm making a mess of this. Look, I just came by to—to tell you that you're off the hook.''

''What?''

Forcing a deep breath into her lungs, Chloe turned to face him. ''It's time to end our charade. Mollie called this morning, begging me to okay the final proof of the invitations. I put her off, but it's not fair to stall her any longer. Or keep you dangling like this.''

''I'm willing to dangle as long as you want.''

She pasted what she sincerely hoped was a smile on her face. ''Really? You weren't dangling a few moments ago. You were practically wrapped around…what was her name?''

''Pam,'' he muttered. ''Pam Hawkins.'' He hesitated, choosing his words with obvious care. ''Look, Chloe, my business with Pam is…complicated.''

''Funny, it didn't *sound* complicated.''

His gray eyes narrowed, and he shot her a look

so swift and sharp and un-Maselike that Chloe blinked.

"What exactly did you hear?"

"Not much," she admitted on a long, gusting sigh. "Only enough to make me thoroughly ashamed of the fact that I've used you."

"I accepted your proposal with my eyes open. You didn't use me."

"Yes, I did, and I'm sorry, Mase. Honestly. I know you assured me that our so-called engagement wouldn't impinge on your private life, but I shouldn't have presumed—I should have realized—I guess I just didn't think things through," she finished miserably.

The elevator door pinged open. Grabbing at the escape it offered, Chloe stepped inside and jabbed the Down button. Mase's hand shot out, catching the door as it started to close.

"We need to talk about this."

"We will. Call me, okay? We'll work out the details of our big breakup." The words left a bitter taste in her mouth. Good grief, what did it take for her to learn her lesson? First she'd let the handsome, debonair Andre con her. Now she'd conned herself into thinking…into hoping…

"No," she said, recanting her offer to talk. "We don't have to work out anything. I shouldn't have risked our friendship by wrapping it in deceit. No more lies, Mase. No more pretense. As of this mo-

ment, you're a free man. Officially, finally and irrevocably.''

His response was a short, pithy curse, something
Chloe wasn't at all used to hearing from him. She
blinked in surprise as he stepped inside the elevator,
caging her against the back wall.

''I'm not letting you walk away until we talk this
through.''

A spurt of temper sliced through her hurt. Her
eyes flashed a warning. ''Back off, mister.''

''Dammit, Chloe...''

''I can't talk about it now. I don't *want* to talk
about it now.''

For a moment she thought he might force the issue. Suddenly, ridiculously, she felt a frisson of
alarm. Not fear, exactly. She couldn't fear Mase if
she tried. Yet this man looked almost like a stranger.
To her infinite relief, he stepped back.

''All right. We'll talk tonight. After the party at
your uncle's house.''

Finally the door whirred shut. Chloe slumped
against the paneled wall, her eyes shut, with Mase's
image blazed on her eyelids. Tall. Dark-haired.
Broad-shouldered. Square-jawed. Smiling down at
Pamela Hawkins, who liked it hard and fast and
rough.

A shiver of revulsion rippled through Chloe, followed immediately by one of pure, undiluted envy.
Mase Chandler certainly hadn't tried anything hard
and fast and rough with her. Face it. He hadn't tried

anything at all. It shattered her to discover that steady, solid Mase possessed a dark side to his character she hadn't even suspected. It shattered her even more to realize that she still wanted him. Desperately.

The elevator zipped downward. With every flashing floor number, Chloe berated herself. How could she be such a fool? When would she learn that she couldn't trust her judgment where men were concerned?

Jaw tight, Mase watched the elevator indicator flash floor after floor. His instincts told him to go after Chloe, to work through this mess before she did something stupid, like announce to her father or brothers or the rest of the Fortune clan that they'd called off their supposedly fake engagement.

Chloe didn't know it, but their engagement had been real from the moment Mase had accepted her ridiculous proposal. For him, anyway. Oh, he'd played by her rules. Kept his hands off her, despite the hunger that had grown in him with every passing day. A hunger that sent him to bed at night hard and aching and determined to finesse his skittish fiancée to the altar.

Now she'd bolted.

He should go after her. Mase knew he should. But the image of her angry, confused face held him back. She said she needed time. Okay. He'd give her time. Until tonight. Then they'd end this charade the way he'd planned to end it all along. With Chloe in his arms and in his bed.

In the meantime, Pam was waiting for him. Blowing out a long breath, Mase raked a hand through his hair. How the hell was he going to explain his convoluted relationship with Pam to Chloe? He couldn't even explain it to himself.

One-time lover? Sometime partner? Friend?

Who was he kidding? The ties that bound them went deeper than that. He and Pam had shared too many hours of danger, too many nights of boredom to qualify as mere friends. He'd have to think of something to tell Chloe, something that didn't violate the absolute security he had sworn to maintain. He couldn't explain about his secret life, the life he'd decided to give up. He couldn't take the same risks, disappear for the same extended periods, as a married man that he did while single. It wouldn't be fair to her...or their marriage.

His mouth twisted. What had she just said? That it was stupid to wrap their friendship in lies and deceit? He wondered what she'd say if she knew they were his stock-in-trade. Or had been until he'd decided to marry her and end his forays into the seamy underworld known as clandestine operations. With a last, frustrated glance at the elevator indicator, Mase spun around and headed back to his office.

Pam had made herself comfortable in the high-backed executive chair behind his desk, her long legs crossed and a rueful smile in her brown eyes.

"Sorry if I made things awkward for you with your fiancée, Mase. Did you soothe her ruffled feathers?"

"I will," he replied with more assurance than he felt at that particular moment. Forcing his thoughts from Chloe to the woman regarding him with cool amusement, he cut back to the reason for her unexpected visit.

"Tell me again why you think Dexter Greene is looking for me?"

Raising a well-manicured hand, Pam ticked off the bare facts she'd related when she'd first arrived less than a half hour ago.

"One, you brought in his son. Two, said son was found dead in his prison cell last month. Three, we sent an operative to the funeral and four, our agent hung around long enough to believe that Dexter Greene's vow of vengeance is more than the ranting of a grief-crazed parent. The father's dangerous, Mase. We knew that when we went in to extract his son."

Frowning, Mase jingled the coins in his pocket. Fractured images of a long, deadly chase flickered through his mind. He could almost hear the pop of gunfire. Taste the coppery residue of fear as he'd slogged through miles of sucking swamp with the gun-running, hate-mongering murderer slung unconscious across his back and Pam panting at his side.

It didn't matter that Greene's son was a con-scienceless bastard. Or that he'd not only supplied stolen weapons to the hate-mongers who'd opened fire on a church full of Asian immigrants, but had planned and participated in the massacre himself. As fanatical about America for Americans as the others in his tight little enclave, the elder Greene no doubt approved of his son's actions.

How the hell had Dexter Greene connected the scruffy, bearded thug who'd snatched his son with the CEO of Chandler Industries?

When he put the question to Pam, she shrugged. "We don't know how he made the initial connec-tion. We *do* know that someone logged on to the computer in the library in Greene's hometown and initiated inquiries about Mason Chandler. We an-swered the queries with the standard cover infor-mation, of course, and sent an operative in to nose around. When he got there, Greene had dropped off the face of the earth."

"Come on, Pam! Our specialty is hostage recov-ery and hostile extractions. We're experts at tracking down the slime no other agency can find. How did our man let Greene slip through his fingers?"

She shrugged again. "I was in the Middle East until two days ago. The Chief called me in when you told him you were out of the business."

"So he sent you to Minneapolis to change my mind."

"Have I?"

"No. I'm getting married in November, remember?"

She cocked a brow. "Are you sure?"

"Pretty sure," Mase replied with a wry smile. "I'll have to do some fast talking in the next few hours to make it happen, though."

"Talking?" The brunette shook her head in mock despair. "That wasn't your style when we worked together. What has this woman done to you?"

Mase wasn't ready to admit that Chloe Fortune had tied him up in knots so tight he'd never unravel them.

"Look, I won't go back into the field, but I'll do what I can to help you with Greene. Did you bring the after-action reports from our original mission?"

"Of course."

"Let me go through them and see if anything shakes out about the father. I'll get in touch with you at your hotel later."

Much later. After he had "talked" to Chloe.

Pam rose with the fluid, feline grace that was hers alone. Slinging the shoulder strap of her calfskin bag over her shoulder, she rounded the edge of the desk and patted him on his cheek.

"I'll be waiting."

By the time Mase wheeled through the open gates of Stuart and Marie Fortune's Minneapolis mansion, the bright fall afternoon had faded into purple dusk. Lights blazed from every window of the two-story stone house belonging to Chloe's uncle. The sound of laughter and chink of glasses carried clearly on the crisp evening air.

From the number of Mercedes and Jags and luxury sports utility vehicles crowding the brick-paved drive, it appeared that the Fortunes had turned out in force tonight for Stuart Fortune's impromptu party. The mysterious invitation, conveyed by Stuart's personal secretary this morning, indicated only that he wanted to welcome a new member of the Fortune family to their midst. At this particular moment, Mase wasn't interested in welcoming anyone. All he wanted was to get face-to-face with his fiancée.

Masking his impatience, he climbed the curving front steps. Moments later he was shown into a high-ceilinged, glass-enclosed palazzo. With its magnificent view of the lakes and the distant city skyline, the sunroom was a favorite gathering spot of the Fortunes. After a quick scan of the crowd, he headed for a familiar figure.

His prospective father-in-law took his hand in a hearty grip. "Hello, Mase. Where's Chloe?"

"She was supposed to meet me here."

"She was?" Emmet Fortune's silvery brows slashed into a straight line. "I wonder what's delaying her."

Having raised Chloe and her twin and their older brother on his own, Emmet's protective instincts kicked into overdrive on a daily, if not hourly, basis.

They were revving up to full power when Chloe's twin strolled over to join them.

For the life of him, Mase couldn't understand how two siblings could look so much alike and possess such different temperaments. They both stopped passersby in their tracks...Chad with his striking Nordic masculinity, Chloe with her breath-stealing, feminine version of her brother's handsomeness. They both kept themselves in superb physical shape with regular and energetic exercise—skiing in winter, swimming and tennis in summer. There the similarities ended. Where Chloe flashed a smile that could melt the ice on Minnesota's lakes in mid-January, Chad's too often held a mocking edge. As it did now.

"Hello, Mase."

"Hi, Chad."

"Chloe asked me to give you something."

Mase stiffened. The hard glint in Chad's violet eyes, so like his sister's, gave him an inkling of what was coming. Sure enough, Chad pulled his hand out of his pocket and uncurled his fingers. A gleaming, emerald-cut diamond lay in his palm.

"She said she forgot to return this to you this afternoon."

His jaw squaring, Mase pocketed the ring. "Where is she?"

Chad didn't try to disguise his hostility. Obviously, his sister had told him about the fiasco at Mase's office this afternoon.

"Gone."

"Gone where?"

"She didn't say. She just indicated that she needed to get away and do some serious thinking."

Emmet broke into the conversation, his fatherly feathers in full ruff. "What the hell's going on here, Mase? Why did you and Chloe call off the wedding?"

"I didn't. Chloe did."

"Why? And what does she have to think about? Dammit, where's my daughter?"

"I don't know, Emmet, but I'll find her."

Chad's smile took on a sharper edge. "I wouldn't bet on it, Chandler. She didn't sound like she wanted finding."

For the first time since he looked up and saw Chloe standing in his office door, Mase felt a flicker of real amusement. None of the Fortunes knew what he did or who he worked for during his extended "business" trips. For security reasons, none ever would.

"I'll find her," he stated with the quiet assurance that came with years of training, a worldwide network of contacts and too many missions to count.

He left the party a few moments later and headed straight for the downtown hotel where Pam was staying. He'd get her working Chloe's license tag and vehicle description with the locals while he tapped into a few restricted networks. It wouldn't take long for him to track down the red, two-seater

Mercedes. When he did, Mase decided grimly, he and his fiancée were going to have that little talk.

They located the Mercedes five hours later. A state trooper had spotted it nose down in a gully some forty miles west of Sioux Falls, South Dakota. The contents of a black leather shoulder bag had spilled onto the floor mat. A fully packed carryall was still in the trunk.

It took almost three weeks to locate the missing driver.

Two

Mase spent those weeks in a blur of long days and endless nights. Controlling the fear that knife-bladed through him each time he thought of the deserted stretch of road and Chloe's crumpled car, he forced himself to work through every possible scenario.

She could have fallen asleep at the wheel and plowed into that ditch. She could have been run off the road by some sex-crazed psycho. Or by kidnappers wanting a piece of her father's wealth. Or, as he grimly discussed with Pam, she could have been followed from his office and snatched by the man who'd sworn vengeance for the death of his son. Mase had to face the very real possibility that he'd been compromised, that Dexter Greene had some-how tracked him down and intended to use his fi-ancée as bait to snare him. The possibility ate like acid through his system.

He sweated blood for almost three weeks. Finally, after hundreds of false leads and dead ends, his agency's far-flung network of contacts paid off. A Seattle-based, long-haul trucker reported picking up a hitchhiker matching Chloe's description during a cross-country run, not far from where her Mercedes was later found. According to the trucker, his pas-senger had sported a good-size lump on her temple and seemed a little dazed. Concerned, he'd taken her to a clinic in Mitchell, South Dakota.

Mase was in the air and en route to Mitchell within thirty minutes of receiving the trucker's re-port. Once there, he picked up Chloe's trail almost immediately. She had arrived at the clinic just minutes after a near hysterical junior high choir di-rector brought in fifteen moaning, vomiting glee club members. In the melee of retching students, frantic parents and harried staff, the emergency room physician examined Chloe, ordered an X ray, diagnosed a mild concussion and released her.

She paid her bill in cash the next day after pawn-ing a sapphire ring. The engraved inscription in the ring, ''To Chloe, with love from Kate,'' provided the first solid proof that Mase was closing in on his missing fiancée.

Then, before the relief and elation at having picked up her trail even peaked, she disappeared again.

It took another twenty hellish hours for Mase to track her from Mitchell to the two-tick town of Crockett, in the southwestern corner of South Dakota. His last report, received just as he was climbing into a helicopter, was that a woman calling herself Chloe Smith had taken up residence with Hannah Crockett, granddaughter of the town's founder and proprietor of the general store.

A late-afternoon sun slanted through the mountain peaks when the helicopter touched down at a prearranged landing site some six miles outside of Crockett.

"I wish you'd let me go in with you," Pam shouted over the whap of the rotor blades.

"I'll signal you if I need backup."

"Dammit, Mase, we still don't know why your fiancée decided to hole up out here, in the middle of nowhere."

He skimmed a quick look at the mountains surrounding them on all sides. Not quite the middle of nowhere, but close.

"Until we do…" Pam yelled.

"Until we do, this is my operation. I'll contact you if I need backup."

Pam sank back against the seat, her mouth a thin

line of disapproval. Mase tipped her a quick farewell and ducked under the whirling blades. A moment later he took the keys of the mud-splashed Chevy Blazer he'd arranged to have delivered to the isolated landing site. The driver shouted quick directions to Crockett before hunching over and dashing to the chopper.

Mase slid into the Blazer and slammed the door on the ear-rattling noise. A quick shake of his leg settled the cuff of his jeans over his scarred boot and the 9mm Glock subcompact it concealed. Smaller and lighter than a snub-nosed Special, the Glock carried a tactical high-velocity load that had helped him out of more than one tight situation.

His face grim, Mase transferred the extra clip and boxes of spare bullets to the Blazer's dash. From the report received just hours ago, it appeared Chloe wasn't under duress. Despite his insistence on going in alone, Mase wasn't taking any chances.

While the helo's engines revved up to full lift power, he pulled a red ball cap from his back pocket and tugged it low on his forehead. In well-worn jeans, a sturdy plaid shirt and blue sleeveless down vest, he'd fit right in with the other hunters and anglers who drove hundreds of miles to hunt game and fish the jewellike lakes that dotted the Black Hills. He had no idea if the sportsman's cover was necessary, any more than he knew why Chloe had chosen Crockett to hide out in. But he intended to find out.

Under the curved brim of the ball cap, Mase's jaw locked tight. He was past feeling the cumulative effects of too little sleep, too many gallons of black coffee and the six kinds of hell he'd gone through since Chloe's disappearance. Even now, despite confirmed reports that she was alive and safe, the mental image of her Mercedes nose down and abandoned in that ditch could still put a kink in his intestines.

He drove the narrow two-lane road, remembering that fear, tasting its bitter residue once again. Now, however, a healthy dose of anger added its own flavor to the fear. At this point, Mase was almost as furious over the torment Chloe had put him and her family through as he was relieved to have found her.

As the Blazer crested a hill dotted with tall pines and dropped down toward the half dozen weathered wooden buildings that comprised Crockett, he couldn't decide whether to hustle her back to Minneapolis or haul her to the nearest motel and stake his claim the way he'd wanted to since the day she proposed to him. He was still debating the issue when he pulled up at the Crockett General Store and killed the Blazer's engine.

Mase climbed out, disappointment rising sharp in his throat. They'd tagged the wrong woman. Chloe couldn't have stayed in this place for almost three weeks! Not his Chloe, anyway.

Eyes narrowed behind his mirrored sunglasses, Mase returned the blank stare of the bleached cow skull mounted above the much-patched screen door. Those weren't the only bones to grace the store. Entwined elk antlers twisted up and around its four wooden porch supports like prickly white ivy.

Against the weathered wood, the antlers were a startling white. In contrast, the rusting South Dakota license plates framing the two front windows provided a riot of color, as did the wooden bins and baskets filled with fall produce that fought for porch space alongside a bagged-ice locker and a bait bucket set under a hand-lettered sign advertising worms and crawlers. The whole weathered wooden structure seemed to list a few degrees to the right, giving the distinct impression that a good wind could topple it over completely.

Warily, Mase mounted the sagging front steps. The boards creaked a protest, but the bell above the door jangled a cheery welcome when he stepped inside. Tangy wood smoke from the cast iron stove in the center of the store caught at his senses along with the equally compelling aromas of fresh-brewed coffee, ripe apples and tobacco.

Mase stopped just inside the threshold, sweeping the store with a searching glance. Enough light filtered through the dust-streaked windows to illuminate the nooks and crannies of the single room, crammed with every imaginable necessity from work boots to cereal to beeswax candles. If there was an order to the jumble of products and produce filling the floor-to-ceiling shelves, he couldn't see it.

Nor did he see anyone resembling Chloe. The tension coiling his body had just torqued up another few degrees when a woman called from a back room.

"I'll be right there."

Relief crashed through him. He would recognize his fiancée's voice in his sleep. Soft and musical, with the rounded Minnesotan vowels that winters in Palm Springs and two years in Paris couldn't erase, it was as much her signature as her silky blond hair and violet eyes.

Still, Mase had to look twice before he recognized the creature who backed bottom-first into the room a few moments later. Bent double, she fishtailed a fifty-pound sack of rock salt along the wooden floor and added it to the others propped haphazardly against the far wall. Mase watched, stunned, as she straightened with a small grunt. Raising an arm, she swiped it across a forehead streaked with sweat and dust.

The face was the same. Classic Chloe, all high cheekbones, creamy skin and full mouth. Her hair was silvery gold, glinting with warmth even scraped back in a no-nonsense ponytail instead of sweeping

to her shoulders in its usual sleek fall. The clothes…
Mase blinked, trying to remember the last time he'd
seen his fiancée poured into thigh-hugging jeans and
a thin yellow T-shirt that displayed a provocative
patch of sweat between her firm breasts…or when
she'd greeted him with such cool, distant politeness.

"Do you want something?"

He went still, thrown off balance for a moment
as much by Chloe's appearance as by her deliberate
remoteness. His every sense alert to possible danger,
he searched the store again. Why was she pretending
not to know him?

The possibilities he'd forced himself to consider
during his long hunt for Chloe leaped instantly to
life once again. Was she trying to warn him? Had
someone forced her to stay in this remote town?
Was she under duress? With a speed that made her
start in surprise, Mase rounded the end of the
counter and edged through the door behind her.

"Hey, you can't go in there!"

Ignoring her startled protest, he did a quick visual
of the storeroom. It held cardboard cartons stacked
almost to the ceiling, several unused display cases
and a jumble of seasonal sporting goods, but no imminent threat that Mase could determine. An open
door in the opposite side wall led to a long, dim
hallway and, presumably, the attached living quarters. Frowning, he spun around to confront a decidedly irate Chloe.

She reached behind him and closed the storeroom door with a snap. ''I don't know what you're looking for, but whatever it is, I'll find it for you. If I can,'' she tacked on in a low mutter.

Slowly, Mase peeled off his sunglasses and stared down at her. If this was an act, it was a damned good one. If not… His gut twisted.

Why would she pretend not to know him? What the hell was going on? He searched her face, her eyes, trying to find a hidden message.

The woman who called herself Chloe Smith lifted her chin and matched the stranger stare for stare. In the almost three weeks she'd lived in Crockett, she'd learned to cope with the kind of looks he was laying on her. As Hannah had dryly pointed out, Chloe was the only nubile young female within fifty miles who didn't come on the hoof. Word that she'd been hired to work the store while Hannah was laid up with multiple fractures to her left ankle had spread faster than a range fire. Every horny cowboy working the ranches around Crockett suddenly found himself needing new work boots or a supply of chewing tobacco. The vet from over at Custer came by twice as often to check the penicillin supplies Hannah kept in the cooler alongside the milk and soda. Even the transient sportsmen who flocked to the area to hunt deer and elk and to fish the mountain lakes had started joining the regulars who clustered around the potbellied stove in the mornings.

Chloe had grown used to being ogled…but that didn't mean she liked it. Especially when the ogler raked her with a pair of iron gray eyes that glittered with an unsettling intensity.

"Did you want something?"

Instead of answering, he shot back a question of his own. "What's going on here?"

Not liking his low growl, she backed up a step. "You tell me."

He followed, too quick and too close for Chloe's peace of mind. Like a hammer striking an anvil, her temple started to throb. The bruise that had marked it had long since faded, but she still suffered from occasional headaches. The accident that caused them remained only a blur in her mind. Vaguely she remembered climbing out of a car and stumbling for miles along a dark, deserted stretch of highway. She could recall the trucker who gave her a ride and the doc who X-rayed her. She couldn't remember who she was, however. Somewhere along that empty stretch of road, she'd lost her identity, her direction and her memory. All she retained were the clothes she was wearing, the sapphire ring that had given her a first name, if not a last, and a vague sense of having run away. From what or from who, she didn't have a clue.

Maybe... Her heart began to echo the pounding in her skull. Maybe from this man.

She eyed him warily. At first glance he didn't look like the kind of man a woman would run from. Tall and muscular, with shoulders that strained the seams of his flannel shirt, he had the healthy tan of an outdoorsman without the weathered, sun-creased skin that characterized so many of the locals Chloe had met. His black brows slashed across a strong brow and defined a face stamped with a hardness she sensed came from within as much as from without. His clothes, she noted, marked him as a fisherman or a hunter. A transient. Here only to bag a trophy kill. She didn't doubt he'd bring down his prey.

Was she his prey? A sudden fear rippled down Chloe's spine. She disguised the shiver with a facade of sheer bravado.

"Back off, mister."

Her brusque warning had just the opposite effect from the one Chloe intended. Instead of putting the stranger on notice, it seemed to spark a flame in his slate gray eyes. Deliberately he took another step forward.

"Back off," she said again.

"Oh, no," he said with a tight little smile. "I think that's been my problem all along. I always back off, when what I really want to do...what I should have done...is this."

Before Chloe could grasp his intent, he wrapped an arm around her waist and hauled her against his chest. She squawked a protest as his mouth came down on hers. Shock held her immobile for a moment or two, just long enough for him to blast through her defensive barriers and shatter her senses.

The searing kiss answered one of the questions whirling around in Chloe's head. She didn't know this man. Or more correctly, she'd never kissed him before. Not like this. There was no way she could have forgotten the rough thrill of his mouth on hers. No way she would have run from the heat his touch flushed in her veins. For an absurd moment she felt as though this kiss was what she had been running *toward* when she'd landed in Crockett.

Then the confusion and wariness that had plagued her for the past few weeks shuddered back. She pushed free of the stranger's hold and stepped away, as furious now as she'd been frightened a moment before.

"Who are you?"

He didn't answer for a long time. Too long for Chloe's thin-stretched nerves. Thoroughly shaken and still seared with anger, she whirled and put the long counter between them.

Her nails dug into the wood. Her voice shook with fury. "Who are you? And what in the blue blazes gives you the right to come on to me like that?"

For a moment the taut planes of his face seemed to shift, become even harder, if that was possible. A frown slashed deep grooves between those coal black brows.

"My name's Mase," he said deliberately. "Mason Chandler."

Chloe tested the name in her mind, willing a spark of recognition. Nothing came. Not even a flicker. Crushing waves of relief and disappointment rolled through her. For a moment there, she'd feared… She'd hoped…

The unmistakable snick of a trigger cocking brought her head snapping around. Across the counter from her, every muscle in the stranger's body seemed to lock. Taut as a steel cable, he turned and stared down the twin barrels of a .12 gauge shotgun.

Three

Her heart hammering, Chloe spun around to face the leathery faced woman who stood with a shotgun cradled under one armpit and a metal crutch propped under the other.

"Hannah!"

The store proprietor didn't take her eyes from the man at the other end of the gun barrel.

"Got a problem here, girl?"

The laconic question shattered the tension that gripped Chloe. More concerned now with the fact that her employer had dragged herself out of bed against her doctor's vehement orders than with her response to the stranger's kiss, she shook her head.

"Nothing I can't handle."

"Funny way of handlin' things, if you ask me," the older woman twanged.

Chloe flushed, but she'd learned that Hannah Crockett's tart tongue came part and parcel with a heart wider than the blue Dakota sky. She'd wandered into town only a few days after the general store proprietor had tumbled off a ladder and crawled into the street on her belly to get help, dragging her shattered ankle behind her. The cantankerous invalid had hired Chloe on the spot to tend the shop while she was laid up. Hannah had brushed aside such piddling trifles as references and identification. She was good at sizin' up people, she informed Chloe testily. It didn't matter a horse's spit where the girl had come from, or where she was driftin' to. The job was hers, if she could handle it. A spare bedroom came with it, and any meals she wanted to fix up. Otherwise, she could order for them both from the café in town.

Chloe had snatched at the offer, assuming that her duties would center primarily on ringing up sales in the old-fashioned brass cash register that dominated the counter. Three weeks and countless hours of stocking shelves, sweeping floors, breaking down boxes and scuttling fifty-pound sacks across the floor had taught her differently. The work was backbreaking and seemingly endless. With the store open from eight in the morning until nine at night, she earned every penny of the salary Hannah paid her in addition to her room and board. She'd also taken on the duties of nurse and companion, despite Hannah's grumbling that she could take care of herself.

Worried by the deep white lines grooved on either side of her reluctant patient's mouth, Chloe hurried around the counter. "We need to get you back to bed. The specialist in Rapid City said you should stay off that ankle until he takes the pins out."

"If I listened to him and laid on my backside for six weeks, I'd sprout carbuncles the size of Idaho potatoes." Keeping the shotgun level with the ease of one used to its heavy weight, she shifted her stance and gave the stranger another once-over. "What did you say your name was?"

"Chandler, Mason Chandler."

"Hmmmm. You go around kissin' up every girl you happen to come across, Chandler, or is there something special 'bout our Chloe here?"

Mase debated how best to answer that one. He'd already blown any need for a cover by giving Chloe his name...not that his real identity seemed to matter to her. The absurd thought occurred to him that she might be putting him through the hoops for the scene in his office with an elaborate pretense of not recognizing him. He dismissed that thought as soon as it formed. To all intents, it appeared Chloe really *didn't* know him.

A trickle of cold sweat formed between Mase's

shoulder blades. His medical training as an under-cover operative had consisted of such useful field techniques as packing gunshot wounds, administering antisnakebite serum and treating frostbite. The little he'd read about amnesia made him hesitant about blurting out her identity. He needed expert medical advice, and fast. In the meantime, he owed Hannah an answer.

"There's definitely something special about Chloe," he said with perfect truth. "Any man with eyes in his head could see that. But I shouldn't have come on to her the way I did."

"Hmm."

The woman's watery blue eyes held his for another second or two, then she lowered the shotgun and uncocked the hammer with an agile flick of her thumb.

"Did that sound like an apology to you, Chloe?"

"Close enough," she bit out, obviously unimpressed. "Come on, Hannah, let's get you back to bed."

"In a minute, girl, in a minute."

The older woman angled a head haloed by short, feathery, white wisps of hair. Her flyaway hair might have given her a pixielike appearance if it hadn't topped a face toughened by wind and sun and shrewd blue eyes.

"So what brings you to these parts, Chandler?"

"Hunting."

"Elk season doesn't start for another two days."

"I thought I'd get in some fishing first."

"You did, did you?"

Impatient now to get to a phone, Mase brought the inquisition to an end. "I came in to buy a fishing permit. I'll come back later, after you get off that ankle."

"I never turn away a payin' customer, boy."

All brisk business now, Hannah laid the shotgun on the counter and hobbled toward a slotted wooden box…or tried to. After only a single step, her crutch hit an uneven patch of floor. Her good leg buckled. She grunted in pain and started to topple backward. Mase caught her just before she hit the hard wooden floor.

With Chloe hurrying ahead to show the way, he carried a muttering, thoroughly disgusted Hannah through the cluttered storeroom and down the hall he'd glimpsed earlier. The hall gave onto a kitchen on one side and a combined living room and office that had been converted into a downstairs bedroom for the invalid. A narrow flight of stairs led, Mase guessed, to the upstairs bedrooms.

Edging sideways to avoid any contact between the bulky cast encasing Hannah's ankle and the door frame, he deposited her gently on the blankets mounded on the sofa. By the time she'd stretched out and propped her leg on a pillow, the blood had drained from her face.

Chloe clucked in concern. "You'd better take one of your pain pills. I'll get some water."

"I'm not taking those damned pills," her patient snapped. "They make me feeble-minded."

"They make you sleepy," her nurse countered, "and rest is exactly what your ankle needs."

Hannah huffed but didn't argue further. Mase waited to excuse himself until Chloe had returned with a glass of water. He had a patient of his own to care for.

"I'll come back for the permit later, when you're not so busy."

Chloe only nodded, but her gaze followed him down the hall. She chewed on her lower lip, fighting an inexplicable urge to call him back.

She hadn't felt the faintest memory stir when he said his name, and she'd stake what little she possessed at this moment on the fact that he'd never kissed her before. Not with that soul-shattering thoroughness, anyway. Yet a flutter of panic grabbed her at the thought that he might walk out of the store and out of Crockett.

Why did she care? Who was he? Oh, God, who was she? More to the point, who was she running from? And why? The same questions that had haunted her for weeks made the hand holding the glass tremble.

"Do you know him, child?"

She swung her gaze back to Hannah's. The un-

derstanding in the weathered face calmed her incip-
ient panic, just as it had so many times in the past
weeks.

"I don't... I can't..." She gave a long, shaky
sigh. "No."

A leathery palm came up to pat her hand. "It's
all right, Chloe. Don't fret. When you're ready,
you'll remember."

"What if I'm never ready?"

"Just take it a day at a time. A day at a time."

She managed a wobbly smile. "Do I have a
choice?"

"Maybe. Maybe not."

A frown wrinkled Hannah's forehead as her
young helper pushed to her feet. She hated the help-
lessness that kept her on this damned sofa, almost
as much as she hated her inability to banish the
shadows from her young friend's eyes.

She'd known since the first moment the slender
blonde in new-bought jeans and a fuzzy yellow
sweater showed up at the store that there was more
to Chloe Smith than a mere drifter. Just as she now
knew there was more to Mason Chandler than a casual hunter. She'd seen enough in her sixty or so
years to consider herself a good judge of horseflesh
and a fair judge of men. For all that this Chandler
fellow's kiss had shaken Chloe right down to her
toes, Hannah's instincts told her he didn't mean
harm by her. She intended to keep a close eye on

the girl, though, just in case…and she'd make damned sure the rest of Crockett's inhabitants kept Chandler in their sights.

"Hand me the phone, girl," she said briskly, her near accident forgotten. "I'll call down to Harold and order us some supper from his diner."

Mase drove Crockett's half-block-long downtown, searching the handful of buildings that fronted the single street for a hotel. The closest he could find was a two-story edifice in silvery wood. Under a shaggy moose head, a weathered sign proclaimed that the building housed the "Offices of the Mayor," the "Dobbins Taxidermy Studio" and the "Crockett Café and Pool Hall." A tacked-on cardboard strip announced rooms to let in hunting season.

Ten minutes later the portly mayor/taxidermist/restaurateur showed Mase to an upstairs room generously decorated with examples of his art. Stuffed rainbow trout and ringtail quail shared wall space with an arched-back bobcat. A stag head with a full rack of antlers was mounted above the narrow bed, at just the right height to stare regally at his reflection in the dresser mirror.

It took some doing, but Mase finally eased his loquacious host out the door, dumped his carryall on the chenille-covered spread and reached for the cell phone he'd tucked in his shirt pocket. Three calls and ten minutes later, Pam Hawkins answered his coded signal.

"Did you find her?"

"I found her," Mase replied grimly. He gave Pam a quick rundown on the situation, then cut right to the reason for the call.

"I just contacted the clinic in Mitchell and told them I was sending a courier to pick up the doctor's report and the X rays they took of Chloe."

"I'll take care of it."

Mase smiled grimly at the flat, no-nonsense response. Now that he'd found his missing fiancée and ascertained that she wasn't in imminent danger, he was stretching things by using his covert contacts like this. Thankfully, Pam had even less concern for such niceties than he did.

"Have the X rays delivered to the Chicago offices of Dr. Peter Chambers. He's standing by, waiting for them."

His partner whistled. "Chambers is one of the top neurologists in the country, isn't he?"

"From all reports."

"Call me back when you hear from him, okay?"

"Will do. And thanks, Pam."

Mase cut the connection, then hefted the small instrument in his hand. His next call would be to Emmet. It wasn't one he looked forward to. Chloe's father had lost both sleep and weight in the past three weeks. Her brothers hadn't fared much better.

Half the Fortune clan, her great-aunt Kate included, had wanted to fly out to Crockett when Mase announced that he'd located his missing fiancée and was going after her.

Not knowing what the situation might be, Mase had persuaded them to stay home until he phoned. Now Mase would have to break the news about Chloe's condition to Emmet.

The call proved every bit as explosive as anticipated. A furious Emmet Fortune singed the ends of Mase's hair, first for instigating whatever damn fool argument had sent his daughter off into the night, then for refusing to take him along when he went to find her. Only the prospect of a three-way conference call with the neurosurgeon kept Chloe's father from slamming the phone down and flying straight out to South Dakota.

They held the conference call three hours later. Dr. Chambers proved as calm and professional as Emmet Fortune was wired.

"I would have preferred to look at a complete CAT scan, but the X rays you sent are surprisingly good. The doctor in Mitchell knew what he was doing."

"The hell he did!" Emmet huffed. "The idiot diagnosed a concussion—a concussion, for God's sake!—then let Chloe wander off on her own."

"He diagnosed a mild concussion," Chambers corrected, "as evidenced by the bruise on her temple. There were no other signs of trauma, nor did your daughter complain of any pain or dizziness when she was seen, only a slight disorientation. She didn't tell the doctor she was experiencing memory loss at the time of her examination."

"Yes," Emmet exploded, "and I want to know why!"

"I'm only speculating at this point, of course, but short-term memory loss is more common that you would imagine in accidents like this. The victims often try to conceal their state. They're confused and frightened by their inability to recall who they are or where they are. Many hope their memory will return if they function as normally as possible."

"Will it?" Mase asked, gripping the phone with white-knuckled intensity. He had a good idea that Emmet was doing the same at his end of the line.

"In most cases, yes. Provided another shock or trauma doesn't cause the victim to retreat even further."

"Another trauma! No one's going to shock or hurt my little girl! Not if I'm alive to stop it."

Mase sidestepped Emmet's furious explosion. "What do you recommend?"

"Don't force her. Let her set the pace of her own recovery."

"Are you saying we shouldn't tell her who she is?" Mason asked.

"Or bring her home?" Emmet sputtered.

Chambers hesitated, but he hadn't made it to the pinnacle of his field by hedging his opinions.

"You said she didn't recognize you, Chandler, and you're her fiancé. The odds are she won't recognize her own name if you provide it. No, at this point, I wouldn't throw her identity at her or make her face a lot of friends and relatives. Give her some time."

"The hell you say," her father shouted. "I want a second opinion."

"You're free to consult with whomever you please," the doctor replied. "I can refer you to a specialist in New York."

His reasonable reply took none of the wind from Emmet's sails. Instead, Chloe's father changed his tack.

"I'm coming out there, Chandler."

Mase gripped the phone, knowing he wasn't about to win any brownie points with his future father-in-law. "Why don't we let the doc off the line, Emmet, then we'll talk about it."

An excruciating fifteen minutes later, Mase snapped the cell phone shut. Emmet was determined to get a second opinion, maybe a third. He'd agreed to stay in Minneapolis—for now!—but he made it clear that he'd nail Mase's hide to his trophy room wall if anything or anyone harmed Chloe further.

With that promise ringing in his ears, Mase debated his next move. The tantalizing aroma of fried onions wafting under the door decided the issue. He couldn't remember downing anything but coffee since the night Chloe disappeared.

He slipped the phone into his vest pocket and headed for the door, only to yank the instrument out again when it hummed against his chest. A quick glance at the incoming number told him the call was secure.

"What's up, Pam?"

"I thought you should know Dexter Greene just surfaced. We got a report that he rented a vehicle under an assumed name at the Minneapolis airport. The car was spotted the next day parked a few blocks from your house."

"The hell you say!"

"We're tracking him, Mase. Or trying to. He's as slippery as his son was, and twice as smart. When are you coming back to help me with this?"

"I'm not. He's all yours."

"What?"

"I'm staying in Crockett for a while. With Chloe."

"Oh. What's the diagnosis?" Pam asked belatedly.

"Dr. Chambers says it may take a while for her to recover her memory."

"Just out of curiosity, how long is a while?"

"However long it takes, I'll be with her."

A small silence was Pam's only answer to that.

Snapping the phone shut a few moments later, Mase followed his nose down the stairs.

He'd grab something to eat, he decided, then head back to the general store. The sign beside the front door said it stayed open until nine. He'd told Chloe he'd come back for his fishing license. It was as good an excuse as any to reestablish contact with her.

Assuming she'd speak to him after his caveman tactics.

Mase couldn't blame anyone but himself for that blunder. He'd been so relieved to find her and so damned hungry for the taste of her mouth that he'd pushed right past the restraints he'd maintained throughout their long engagement.

Now he faced a whole new set of restraints. He couldn't touch her, much less taste her, until her memory returned. Or, he thought grimly, he won her trust. Either way, the next few days or weeks or months could prove even tougher than the past year had.

The prospect put tight lines beside his mouth as he walked into the combination pool hall, bar and café.

"Grab a stool," Mayor Dobbins called cheerfully from his position in front of the grill. One-handed, he reached into the cooler behind the counter and slid a long-neck across the counter. "I'll get your order as soon as I finish up this order of onions for Miz Hannah. She likes 'em sizzling.''

Under the watchful eyes of a curly horned mountain goat, Mase straddled a stool and took a long, grateful pull of beer. Lowering the half-emptied bottle, he sniffed appreciatively at the heaping mounds of succulent onions and crisp fried liver.

''Does Hannah come in here to eat?''

''She did before she busted her ankle,'' Dobbins answered with a shrug. ''Since she's been laid up, though, Chloe fetches her dinner for her.''

''She does, huh?'' Mase twirled his beer thoughtfully. ''Why don't I spare the lady a trip and take their dinner up to the store? You can add another order of that liver and onions for me, too.''

The mayor complied, chuckling as he tossed a slab of raw liver onto the grill. ''I hope you're not thinking about a cozy little picnic with Miz Hannah and Chloe. The one's too tart to put up with such foolishness, and the other...''

''The other?''

Dobbins sent a cloud of onions into the air with a flip of his spatula. ''Well, let's just say you aren't the only male around these parts with picnics and such on his mind, Chandler.''

A frown snaked between Mase's brows. Before he could demand an explanation, the mayor's cheerful grin faded.

''Not that Chloe pays any attention to the randy

young goats who've come sniffing around her. Someone's hurt that girl. Bad.''

He swung around and jabbed his spatula in Mase's direction. The abrupt movement sent an arc of onions flying across the counter. They landed with a splat on his customer's blue down vest, but Dobbins didn't seem to notice. His chubby face had hardened into lines of fierce protectiveness.

''There are some of us in Crockett who wouldn't take kindly to seeing her hurt again.''

''You can count me among them.''

Dobbins studied him a moment longer before nodding and turning back to his grill. Thoughtfully, Mase picked the onions off his chest and popped them into his mouth, then downed a second beer while he waited. He wasn't surprised that the mayor and the feisty general-store proprietor had taken Chloe under their wing. Her breezy smile alone had won more hearts than Mase's.

As soon as Dobbins bagged up the dinner orders, Mase snatched it up with the instructions to add the total to his bill. Impatience to see Chloe again gnawed at his insides even more sharply than his now-ravenous hunger.

Once out in the swiftly falling dusk, he opted to walk the fifty or so yards to the general store. Crockett didn't boast any sidewalks, only the road that ran straight through town. His long legs ate up the blacktop, while his lungs dragged in sharp mountain night air. An owl hooted in the distance. The lonely howl of a coyote answered a few seconds later.

Within minutes, Mase reached the Crockett General Store. He had to admit the place looked better at night. The full moon hanging just above the granite peaks that surrounded Crockett gave the weathered storefront a silvery sheen. Warm, golden light streamed through its dusty windows. Even the crates and bins piled on the crowded porch held a special…

Mase froze, searching the shadows at the far end of the porch. His body went wire tight as he caught another flicker of movement. He barely had time to assimilate the glint of moonlight on pale blond hair before Chloe's agonized shriek tore through the night.

Four

With Chloe's scream echoing in his ears, Mase re-
acted instinctively. The paper bag in his hand went
flying. In a single fluid movement, he bent, yanked
the Glock from its leather ankle holster, thumbed the
safety and launched himself toward the shadows of
the porch. His shin slammed into a wooden crate. A
bushel basket of potatoes got in his way. He kicked
it aside and jumped a tangle of new rope before he
got to the frantic figure at the far end of the porch.

"Oh, God! Oh, God! Oh, God!"

She danced away from him, her face contorted.
Mase's heart almost clawed through his rib cage as
he searched the shadows for an unknown, unseen

threat, all the while following her erratic passage across the porch.

"What is it? Chloe, what's the matter?"

"Oh, God!"

"What happened! Tell me!"

The whiplike command finally penetrated. Scrubbing her hands up and down the front of her jeans, she jerked out a reply. "I was...reaching for the switch on the ice locker...and I stuck my hand...in the bait box!"

"What?"

"The worms!" she wailed. "I stuck my hand in the damned worms!"

Mase gaped at her. His blood thundered in his ears. Every muscle in his body screamed with the need to act, to shield, to protect. He'd left all remnants of his cool in the street with the liver and onions and charged across the porch to rescue Chloe from night crawlers.

Luckily she was too absorbed with scrubbing her palm down her jeans to notice either his gun or his total lack of cool. Willing his pulse to something less than mach-three airspeed, Mase thumbed the safety again and slid the Glock into its leather nest.

"Oh, yuck! I've got dirt and gunky stuff all over me!"

Shuddering and stamping her feet, she started to dance again. Mase caught her elbow and steered her toward the window.

"Move into the light. I'll de-worm you."

He squatted in front of her and dusted his hands down her legs, dislodging a few squiggly critters in the process. With a disgusted "arrrgh," Chloe stamped a couple more times. The potatoes Mase had knocked over bumped across the boards. He ran his hands down her legs and across her sneakers a final time.

"You're clean."

"Not hardly." Shuddering, she slumped against the windowsill. "Ugh! I have a feeling I'm going to dream about creepy crawlies tonight."

Mase dangled his wrists on his bent knees and battled a grin. Not very successfully, as it turned out. Chloe caught his expression and gave a little huff.

"You wouldn't think it was so funny if those slimy things had been crawling down your leg."

"No, I guess not."

He wiped the grin off his face, but couldn't resist the urge to pull her chain just a bit. She looked so thoroughly and completely disgusted.

"Worms aren't so awful. In fact, they're kind of interesting when you consider that they lack lungs or gills, but can breathe underground and underwater."

"Interesting to you, maybe."

"Did you know the average earthworm's body is divided into about a hundred and fifty segments?

Each segment moves independently to propel it forward.''

She glared at him. ''What are you, some kind of a wormophile?''

The grin snuck back. ''Nope. But I did have a heck of a crush on my high school biology teacher. Mrs. Bellario…every teenage boy's dream come to life.''

Chloe huffed again. ''Let me guess. Beautiful, smart, and as well endowed as they come.''

''You got it.''

He pushed to his feet, fighting a sense of wry disbelief. None of the scenarios that he'd envisioned might occur after he located Chloe included dusting her down for worms or discussing his long-ago lust for the curvaceous Mrs. Bellario. Nor had he envisioned finding his sophisticated fiancée in cheap sneakers, even cheaper jeans and a long-sleeved white T-shirt that displayed many of South Dakota's tourist attractions.

Her attractions, as well, Mase noted with a sudden punch that destroyed any inclination to continue his teasing. The light streaming through the window behind her left her face in shadow but picked up every curve, every indentation of her slender body. The desire he'd banked for so long hit him square in the chest.

He reached out a hand, his throat tight. Maybe if he just talked to her. Just talked to her.

"Chloe..."

"I'm okay now. Slimy, but okay." She scrubbed her palm down her jeans one last time and sent him a rueful smile. "Thanks, Mr. Chandler."

It was another hit to the chest. Sharper. Far more direct.

"Mase," he said slowly. "The name's Mase."

"Thanks, Mase." She tilted her head, studying his face in the light from the window. "And thanks for catching Hannah this afternoon."

From the reluctant gratitude in her voice, Mase gathered that his timely save had won him a measure of forgiveness for his caveman tactics earlier.

"You're welcome. I'm just glad I was close enough to catch her."

"Me, too. The last thing she needs is another fall."

"Is that what happened? She fell?"

"Right off the top step of the ladder. She was checking the shelf life on the cereal boxes."

"That sounds like a dangerous occupation for a woman her age."

"I guess you came back for your fishing permit," Chloe said, shoving off the windowsill. "Come inside. I'll wash up and write out the permit for you."

"That wasn't the only reason I came back," he admitted as he righted the bushel basket he'd toppled in his charge across the porch. "I brought your dinner. There are a couple of orders of liver and onions lying around here somewhere."

Her low gurgle of laughter cut right into Mase. She sounded so much like herself that his stomach did a quick two-step with his backbone.

"So that's what I smell. For a minute there, I wasn't sure if it was me or the worms or..."

"Or me?"

"Well..." She sniffed delicately. "The aroma did sort of follow you."

This just wasn't his night, Mase decided. He searched behind him for the sack he'd tossed aside when he'd reached for his weapon. "I'm afraid our dinner landed in the dirt with the worms."

"*Our* dinner?"

"Mayor Dobbins threw in an extra order," he replied blandly. "I haven't eaten in a while, and my stomach was rumbling loud enough to get a glassy-eyed stare from the mountain goat above the grill."

As if to prove his point, the organ under discussion gave a long, protesting growl.

"I'll go back down to the café for another order while you wash up," Mase offered.

"Never mind. Liver and onions aren't exactly my favorite item..."

His pulse jumped. How did she know that? How much did she recall of her likes and dislikes? Was she starting to remember?

"...from Harold's menu," she finished with a

shrug, unaware of his sudden stillness. "Hannah and I will make do with sandwiches tonight."

"I'm not real high on fried liver, either. Sandwiches sound good to me."

He was pushing. Chloe knew it and didn't particularly like it. He could see the hesitation in her face, hear it in her grudging invitation.

"Come inside, then. You can keep Hannah company while I wash up and raid the cold cuts."

The much-patched screen door squeaked on its hinges, as did the glass-fronted door behind it. The color and jumble of the store reached out to grab Mase as soon as he followed Chloe inside. Although he was seeing the rows of shelves crammed with goods for the second time, the eye-dazzling display still hit him with the visual equivalent of a stun gun.

"Do the residents of Crockett ever need an item that this store doesn't carry?"

Chloe skimmed a look around the jam-packed shelves. "If they do, they haven't asked me for it yet."

"Is that so? How long have you been working here?"

Her smile faltered at the casual question, then disappeared completely. The skin over her cheekbones seemed to tighten.

"Awhile. Come on. We'll let Hannah know you're here, then I'll wash up."

Mase followed her through the storeroom to the

living quarters at the back of the store. He had no difficulty interpreting her evasive reply or the stiff set to her shoulders. The message came through loud and clear. She didn't trust him. Not enough to talk about her apparent amnesia, anyway.

After this afternoon, he couldn't blame her. He still had a way to go before he completely recovered from that blunder. And, he thought grimly, from the scene in his office. When Chloe's memory returned, she'd demand an explanation. Mase had one ready, one that didn't breach security, but the idea of lying to her again left a coppery taste in his mouth.

Damn! How had his relationship with Chloe gotten so bogged down in deceit? He hadn't deliberately set out to mislead her. He'd been working for the government for years before she returned from Paris and burst into his life. He'd conducted a couple of particularly dangerous missions during their long engagement, but he'd made the conscious decision to end his career as an undercover agent. It wasn't fair to Chloe for him to lead a second life that regularly put him in the line of fire, even if she didn't know anything about that life. Still, there was no getting around the fact that he'd lied to her by omission.

The same could be said of their phony engagement. True, it had been Chloe's idea, not his. But he'd certainly taken advantage of the opportunity she'd handed him to finesse her closer and closer to the real thing. Another few days, a couple of weeks at most, and they would have peeled back the layers of lies and subterfuge to the core of friendship and desire that bubbled beneath.

So here he was, Mase thought with an ironic twist of his lips, perpetuating another deceit. Pretending he didn't know Chloe. Keeping his distance and his silence, when everything in him wanted to cradle her in his arms, to soothe away the confusion and fear she must be feeling.

He was beginning to appreciate just how tough the next few days or weeks might be when Chloe led the way into the living room.

"Hey, Hannah," she called with a forced cheerfulness that dug at his heart. "Mase is here."

From her nest of hand-sewn quilts, the older woman flicked him a considering glance. If she made any special note of Chloe's use of his first name, she didn't comment on it.

"He brought our dinner from the café, but it ended up in the dirt, along with half your stock of night crawlers."

"That so?"

"I'll let him explain. I have to clean up, then I'll throw together some sandwiches."

While Chloe's footsteps echoed on the wooden stairs, Hannah waved a hand toward the overstuffed armchair on the other side of the pine coffee table. "Have a seat, Chandler. I have to admit, I'm a bit curious about just how you came to be feedin' my dinner to the worms. I'm curious about a few other matters, too.''

Mase settled his weight on the lumpy cushion. The speculative look Hannah laid on him said more clearly than words that she didn't quite trust him, any more than Chloe did. It also told him that he was in for a tough inquisition. Not that he doubted his ability to dodge any questions that cut too close to the truth. Mase still carried the scars from his decidedly uncomfortable session with the Colombian dopers who'd tried unsuccessfully to break his cover a couple of years ago.

He had to admit that he hadn't exactly anticipated spending the first hours after he'd found Chloe dodging her protector's questions, though. Or sharing sandwiches in a small, cluttered living room. His earlier plans to sweep his fiancée off to the nearest hotel came back to mock him. Images rolled through his mind in vivid Technicolor. Of Chloe smiling her understanding when he explained away Pam. Of Chloe flushed with passion when he kissed her with none of the restraint he'd shown all these months. Of Chloe naked, panting, wanting him as much as he wanted her.

With a silent, frustrated sigh, Mase filed the images away for another day. Another night.

Sure enough, Hannah waited only until the sound of Chloe's footsteps had faded before dismissing any polite chitchat with a wave of a hand misshapen by arthritis.

"Just between you and me, Chandler, what I want to know is what brought you to Crockett…and what, exactly, you're hunting."

"I came to find Chloe."

"Why?"

"Because she's my fiancée."

"Hmm."

"You don't sound particularly surprised."

"Maybe that's because I'm not," Hannah retorted. "I figured Chloe was either your wife or about to be. I also figured that it was only a matter of time until someone came looking for her. So why'd she run away from you?"

The best cover, Mase had learned over the years, required the least subterfuge. Elaborate details and complex identities could trip a man under questioning…particularly the Colombian brand of questioning.

"She walked into my office and found me with another woman in my arms."

Mase didn't make any excuses or apologies. Those he owed to Chloe, and only to Chloe. Folding her hands across the blankets, Hannah contemplated him with about as much warmth as her employee had given the night crawlers.

"You're lucky she just ran away, Chandler. From what I've seen of that girl in the past few weeks,

she's got enough grit in her gullet to grab my shotgun and blow you from here to next year if she takes
a mind to.''

"I'm going to do my damnedest to see she
doesn't take a mind to.''

"Hmm.''

There was no mistaking the message in the single,
drawn-out syllable. If he hurt Chloe again, inten-
tionally or otherwise, Hannah would take matters
into her own hands.

"Why haven't you told her who she is? Or who
you are?''

"After I found her this afternoon and realized she
didn't recognize me…''

"After you kissed her and she didn't recognize
you, you mean,'' the gray-haired woman said with
a snide smile. "That creased your ego a mite, didn't
it?''

"Let's just say it spurred me to consult with one
of the top neurosurgeons in the country. I talked to
him for some time after I left here. He recommends
letting Chloe find her own way back, at her own
pace.''

"What about her family? Did they agree?''

"Reluctantly.''

Mase didn't even bat an eye at that gargantuan
understatement.

"So you're not going to tell her anything?''

"Not until she asks.''

"That right? What if she never asks?"

"I'll worry about never when it comes," he replied grimly.

Hannah was silent for several moments. Mase had just decided that the inquisition was over when her mouth cracked into a tight smile.

"Well, I'll tell you this, boy. Chloe Smith came here about as ignorant of the workings of a country store as anyone ever was, but she's learned fast, damned fast. She's studied up on the business and cleaned the place up as much as I'd let her. She gives me nightly tallies of sales and expenses, not that I do anything with the dad-blamed things. She's even got the mule-headed route man who's been squeezin' my profit margin on beer and wine agreeing to cut his wholesale prices."

"That doesn't surprise me. Chloe comes from a family of remarkable businessmen. She's spent the past year or so developing her own sales and marketing skills."

"Her sales and marketing skills aren't all she brought along with her to Crockett," Hannah drawled. "Every ranch hand within a hundred miles who isn't dead from the waist down or hat-over-heels in love with his horse has been tryin' to snare her interest. Business hasn't been this good since before that supermarket went in over at Custer."

That didn't surprise Mase, either. Chloe's smile could light up Minneapolis in the dead of winter.

The idea that it was lighting up a number of the locals didn't particularly sit well with him, however. He was trying to digest the tight curl of displeasure in his gut when Hannah leaned forward, her eyes dead serious.

"What I'm telling you, Chandler, is that I wouldn't mind one little whit if Chloe decided to stay here in Crockett. Permanently."

Mase's jaw tightened. "*I* would."

"Right now," she drawled, sinking back against the sofa cushions, "your druthers don't matter a lick of spit to me. They matter even less, it appears, to the woman upstairs."

Chloe gave herself far more time than she needed to clean up and change. Her jeans went into the antique egg crate she'd appropriated from the storeroom to use as a hamper. So did the long-sleeved T-shirt. Resisting the urge to shower away all traces of her close encounter with the worms, she settled for some serious scrubbing with a scratchy washcloth. That done, she padded into the spare bedroom under the slanting eaves and pulled a clean top and jeans out of the bureau that held her few changes of clothing. Hannah had insisted that she take whatever she needed from the supply of gaudy T-shirts and sweatshirts they stocked for the tourists, but Chloe hadn't wanted to abuse her employer's generosity. Nor had she wanted to spend more than absolutely necessary of the salary she was carefully hoarding...just in case she found herself alone and lost again.

Shivering, Chloe slammed the bureau drawer shut. It took only a moment or two to tug on the clothes and drag a brush through her hair, but a reluctance to leave the tiny bedroom with its handcrafted, lodgepole pine furniture kept her standing before the bureau. The room had become her sanctuary. Here she'd learned not to panic at the shadows that darkened her mind. Here, in the bed Hannah's grandfather had made with his own hands when he first settled the area, she'd forced herself to accept the bare facts that defined her.

She'd run away from someone or something.

She'd had an accident.

She'd pawned a sapphire ring that someone named Kate had given her and used the money to get as far as Crockett.

Unless, Chloe thought bleakly, she'd found or stolen the ring. In which case, even the name she was using belonged to someone else.

She stared at her own image in the mirror. Who was she? Who had she run from? A familiar panic fluttered in her veins. She fought it, as she had so many times in the past few weeks, gulping in deep breaths.

She wasn't alone. She had to remember that. Hannah had taken her in and showed her a gruff, protecting friendship. Mayor Dobbins and Doc Johnson and the others in the area had accepted her without questions. She felt safe here. Even more important, she felt needed and wanted.

Chloe had no idea why that mattered, or why dealing with suppliers and balancing the day's receipts to the penny and nursing Hannah should give her this sense of satisfaction. Had she led such an empty life before she arrived in Crockett? Had no one ever depended on her, or expected her to put in the kind of back-breaking hours necessary to keep the shelves stocked and the store open from morning till night?

Had no one loved her?

Had she never loved anyone?

Unexpectedly, an image of Mase Chandler, hunkered down on his heels, his mouth tipped into a grin, flashed into her head. Her breath hitched as something tugged at her. She tried to grab it, to pull it out of the haze in her mind. When she finally brought it into the light, her face heated.

It wasn't a memory. It was a need. An undeniably sexual need. She wanted Mase to grin up at her again. Almost as much as she wanted to kiss him again. The sudden contraction low in her belly was lust. Simple, undeniable lust.

Blowing out a long sigh, she addressed the disgruntled image in the bureau mirror.

"Great! Just great! Your mind is mush, but everything from the neck down appears to be functioning normally. You'd better watch yourself around this guy, Chloe Whoever-you-are."

With that stern admonition, she left her sanctuary. A moment later, she breezed past the living room on her way to the store.

"Sorry I took so long. Hang tight while I raid the deli case."

Mase pulled in his long legs and started to rise. "Can I help?"

"No, thanks. Just keep Hannah company. I'll be right back."

The now-familiar scent of smoldering pine logs along with the sharp smell of coffee left too long in the pot greeted her when she stepped into the store. Chloe dumped the dregs and brewed a fresh pot before retrieving Swiss cheese, sliced ham and a paper-wrapped package of smoked venison from the refrigerator case.

She nibbled on a slice of the tangy meat while she sliced the cheese, wondering if she'd ever tasted smoked venison before coming to Crockett. If not, she was certainly hooked on it now. She had just grabbed a loaf of fresh bread from the shelf when the bell above the front door jangled. The man in the curly beard and bulky sheepskin vest who stepped inside greeted her with a shy smile.

"Hello, Chloe."

"Hello, Doc. We didn't expect you today."

"I was out at the Parker place and, uh, thought I'd swing by on my way back to Custer."

Chloe had only lived in the area for a few weeks, but even so she knew that Doc Johnson had driven close to fifty extra miles to "swing by" on his way home. She swallowed a sigh, sincerely hoping he wasn't going to press her for a date again. As nice as he was, she didn't want to go out with him, or with any of the others who'd asked her. Not yet. She wasn't ready.

Or was she?

What about that little pull she'd felt earlier? That tug of sexual need? Chewing on her lower lip, Chloe slanted a quick look at the doc. He was younger than Mase Chandler. More boyish looking, with his mop of sandy curls. His bushy beard utterly failed to give him the air of maturity he obviously tried for. He was younger and nicer and, she sensed with sure, feminine instinct, safer.

"How's Hannah?"

The question brought her wandering thoughts back in focus with a snap. "She was doing better until she got out of bed this afternoon."

"What! The orthopedic specialist in Rapid City ordered her to stay off that ankle for at least six weeks."

"I remind her of that fact at least eight times a day, but she doesn't pay any more attention to me than she does to him." Chloe sent him a worried look. "Her ankle gave way under her, Doc."

"Did she fall again?" he asked sharply.

"No, Mase caught her."

"Mase?"

"A customer. Will you talk to her? Please? Tell her she has to take it easy?"

"She's not my patient, Chloe," he reminded her with a rueful smile. "I could lose my license if I gave her medical advice."

"I know, I know, but you could talk to her as a friend."

"Ha! As if she'd take my advice. I'm still a grubby-faced kid to her. Every time I come in to visit, she reminds me of the time she caught me snitching candy and fed me a dozen dill pickles to teach me a lesson."

Chloe's laughter tinkled through the store. "Poor baby. Did they pucker you up?"

"Permanently." His smile spread into a teasing grin. "Lean across the counter and I'll show you."

Her breath caught in her throat. She met his friendly, hopeful blue eyes and told herself she could do this. She could lean forward and kiss Ted. She *should* do it, if only to prove that Mase Chandler's mind-numbing kiss earlier this afternoon wasn't all that special. He'd simply reawakened feminine instincts that had gone dormant for some reason. She was sure she'd feel the same spark, the same tug with nice, safe Ted Johnson if she just let herself. Slowly she leaned forward.

''What the hell!...''

The exclamation froze Chloe in mid-bend. She slewed her head sideways and met Mase's thunderous gaze.

A door edged open in her mind an inch, maybe two. Not enough for her to see behind it. Only enough for her to turn forward again and calmly brush her lips across Ted's.

Five

It was a pleasant kiss. A friendly, casual contact. Chloe might even have enjoyed it if she hadn't been so conscious of Mase's thunderous scowl...and of the difference between this kiss and the one she'd shared with him earlier that afternoon.

She broke the contact, more than a little ashamed of using Ted Johnson as an experiment. She compensated for her pinprick of guilt by giving him a bright smile.

"Yep, that's some pucker. And to think you owe it all to Hannah."

He answered with a shy smile of his own, but his face held a hint of wariness when he turned toward the man standing in the doorway. Chloe could understand his nervousness. Mase no longer appeared thunderous, merely menacing. He practically bristled, reminding her of a sleek black bear with its fur up, its shoulders hunched and its dinner in imminent danger of scampering away.

His fierce scowl made her nervous, too, but not, she noted with a tingle of surprise, afraid. Tucking that interesting bit of information away in the back of her mind to think about later, she set out to defuse what could fast become an awkward situation. She'd gained enough experience handling the love-hungry cowboys who came into the store to inject just the right mix of casualness and cool into her voice.

"Doc, this is Mase Chandler. He's come up to do some fishing from…?"

Realizing that she had no idea where he called home, she arched an inquiring brow.

"Down," he corrected, his gray eyes tight on her face. "I've come down from Minneapolis."

"Down from Minneapolis," she finished, her smile firmly in place. "Mase, this is Ted Johnson, Dr. Ted Johnson."

Their handshake was a civilized enough ritual, one that men performed every day. Still, Chloe couldn't erase the sensation that a dangerous, untamed animal had reached out to enfold Ted's paw. The young doc was obviously thinking along similar lines. Beneath the short, curly beard, his Adam's apple bobbed up and down.

"Chandler."

"Johnson."

The brief handshake over, Ted made a valiant effort at conversation. "So you're here to fish?"

"And hunt."

"That's right. Elk season starts in a few days. Have you scouted out your stand?"

"Not yet."

Ted ran on for a few minutes about the excellent stands available to rent in the area. Chloe could tell the exact second Mase decided he didn't pose a serious threat. His eyes lost their flinty edge. Imperceptibly his powerful shoulders relaxed.

"You're making late rounds," he commented when the young doc finished.

"Oh, I'm not— That is, I didn't come by to see Hannah. Well, I did, but not…"

Chloe took pity on him. "Doc Johnson's a vet, Mase, not a physician. We sell some of the products that his patients need here in the store."

"So you stopped by to check stock levels, Doc?"

"Well, I— That is—" He pulled his gaze from Mase and screwed up his courage. "Actually, Chloe, I came by to see if you wanted to drive over to Custer State Park tomorrow for the annual buffalo roundup. They're bringing the summer crop of calves down from the hills for shots and ear tagging.''

''Thanks, Ted, but I can't leave Hannah.''

Actually, she could. Her employer had barked at her often enough to get out in the sun and the mountain air. Hannah insisted she could hear the store bell from her sofa. She had enough lung left in her to yell out to any customers who might come in and instruct them to bring their business back to her.

Chloe didn't trust the woman to keep to her sofa, though. Nor did she want to encourage the young vet any more than she already had. She shouldn't have kissed Ted. Shouldn't have hoped for another taste of the desire Mase Chandler had unexpectedly stirred in her this afternoon. Her life was complicated enough right now. She'd be crazy to let her emotions run wild when her memory had come to a complete and total standstill.

Despite her best intentions to nip Ted's interest in the bud, his crestfallen expression tugged at her conscience. That and the fact that he'd driven so many miles out of his way.

''I was just about to make some sandwiches for supper,'' she told him. ''Why don't you join us?''

His blue eyes lit up. ''Is that Mayor Dobbins's latest batch of smoked venison?''

''Yes.''

''Great! Count me in.''

She turned to Mase, keeping her friendly smile

firmly in place. "How about you? Venison or ham and cheese?"

"I'll try the local specialty."

"Good. Ted, you get the drinks. Hannah will have coffee...decaf, but don't tell her! Me, too. Mase, you're in charge of pickles and potato chips."

As he scavenged among the crowded shelves, Mase buried the last remnants of his urge to wipe the pine floorboards with the young vet. The kid didn't constitute any kind of a threat, to him or to Chloe.

Still, it shook Mase to realize how close he'd come to losing his composure, not once, but twice tonight. Charging across the porch to rescue his fiancée from night crawlers had put a serious enough dent in his customary cool. Seeing her lean forward to kiss the curly bearded vet had just about cracked it wide-open.

For a moment there, when Chloe had slewed her head around to meet his stunned gaze, then calmly proceeded to kiss the doc, he'd almost convinced himself that she'd decided on a little payback for the scene with Pam in his office.

On reflection, he shrugged the thought aside. Chloe couldn't stare at him with such wary confusion in her eyes one moment, and deliberately put him through the hoops the next. She wasn't that good an actress.

Was she?

Without being obvious about it, Mase studied her for the next hour or so with the hooded interest of a hawk circling its prey. She said little as they ate, letting the others carry the conversation. Nor did she send so much as a flicker of anything other than polite friendliness his way. If Mase hadn't caught a glimpse of the bleak torment that clouded her eyes for a few seconds at Johnson's offhand reference to his family in Sioux City, his doubts might have taken root.

No, he decided with a twist of his heart. No way she was faking this. Once more he battled an almost-overwhelming urge to gather her in his arms and soothe her fears. Maybe the neurosurgeon had it wrong. Maybe Mase ought to take Chloe home, or at the very least, bombard her with names and images from her past.

Each time he came close to doing just that, though, Hannah's drawled observation echoed in his mind. His druthers didn't matter in this particular situation. Only Chloe's. Even with that constant reminder, he had to force himself to his feet when she rose, gathering the remnants of their picnic supper.

"You've got a long drive yet tonight, Doc," she said in cheerful dismissal. Her glance slid to Mase. "And I expect you'll want to get up with the sun. One of the regulars who came in yesterday said the trout were rising up at Sylvan Lake."

Mase would get up with the sun, all right, but not

to fish. His first priority was to familiarize himself
with the town and the surrounding terrain.

"Sylvan Lake?" he replied with a smile of
thanks. "I'll check it out."

He left a few moments later, a newly issued permit tucked in his wallet. Declining the doc's offer
of a lift to the café, he lingered in the shadows as
the store lights flickered out one by one. Finally only
the glow from the coolers and the red-and-black
neon beer sign in the window cast their glow into
the night.

Turning his back on the darkened store, Mase
walked away from the woman calling herself Chloe
Smith. It was one of the hardest things he'd ever
done in his life.

Dawn brought with it the kind of fall morning that
Mayor Dobbins insisted only the Black Hills of Dakota could produce. Mist lay soft and hazy in the
valley, while the granite peaks surrounding Crockett
thrust into a sky so blue it seemed to sing. Mase
carried a steaming container of coffee out to the
Blazer, almost burning himself when the call of a
bull moose split the morning stillness. The long, rau-
cous cry came from the treeline that climbed the
hills just behind the café/pool hall/taxidermy studio.
From the sound of it, the animal was in full rut.

He wasn't the only one, Mase thought grimly as
he belted himself into the Blazer. Chloe had hit the

nail on the head yesterday when she'd accused Mase of the same rampaging urges. A night's reflection hadn't improved the situation, either. During the agonizing weeks he'd searched for Chloe, Mase had been so damned sure that once he found his missing fiancée the phony engagement could be turned into a real marriage. If only Chloe would forgive his deception.

Well, he'd found her. And now the desire that had left him hard and aching the past few months had gained an added spur. The fierce need drove him to hover over her, to protect her and comfort her when the bleakness he'd glimpsed so briefly last night darkened her eyes to a deep, bruised purple. Mixed up in there as well was the atavistic male urge to stake his claim in a way that overeager puppies like the young vet couldn't miss.

It took some swallowing to digest the fact that Chloe didn't want his protection or his comfort. That disconcerting fact lingered in his mind as he keyed the ignition and shoved the Blazer into gear, then drove up into the hills. It stayed with him while he surveyed the town from the turns along the narrow, twisting road. It dragged at his concentration when he spied lakes and streams that shouted to the angler in him, and brought him back down from the hills when the sun was at its noon brightest.

He parked in front of the general store this time, beside a dented Chevy truck with more mud on its side panels than paint. The scent of freshly brewed coffee pulled him into the store…along with the silvery shimmer of Chloe's laughter. She smiled a welcome when he stepped inside, then returned her attention to the lanky ranch hand standing with stubby pencil and clipboard in hand.

"No, Buck, feminine companionship is *not* one of the survey choices."

"Well, shoot, Chloe, it ought to be."

Great, Mase thought in wry resignation. Another admirer. Hannah certainly hadn't exaggerated the crowd her helper was drawing into the store. To his relief, his fiancée didn't encourage this one to lean across the counter, much less kiss her.

"Just mark those items you think you might need in the next three months," she instructed firmly.

"I need *you*, darlin'." Her customer hung a lonesome look on his face. "I've already waited most of my life for someone like you to come along. Don't think I can wait another three months."

"Sure you can. Finish the survey, Buck."

"Yes'm."

Taking his clipboard and his long look with him, Buck settled in one of the chairs pulled up to the potbellied stove. He propped a worn boot heel on the stove fender, caught his tongue between his teeth and went to work with the stubby pencil.

When Mase strolled over to the counter, Chloe

greeted him with another clipboard and the casual observation that he hadn't fished very long.

"Long enough," he replied easily, skimming the long, handwritten list of products that appeared to include everything from cough drops to motor oil. "What's this?"

"A customer survey."

"A survey, huh?"

Judging from the exchange he'd just overheard, he could only imagine the results she'd get.

"You gave me the idea," she informed him.

"I did?"

"Last night, when you asked if the residents of Crockett ever needed anything that the store didn't carry. I thought about that after I went to bed."

That put him squarely in his place, Mase thought dryly. He'd lain awake worrying about Chloe all night. She'd lain awake worrying about the store.

"I think Hannah's stocked up on every item her customers have ever asked for," she said, her brow knitting. "We've got dozens of items that haven't moved at all in the weeks I've been here. Those onesies and twosies of items eat up valuable shelf space. Hannah hates change, but I'm hoping this survey will convince her to stock more of what sells, instead of what *might* sell."

"By asking the customers what they really need, as opposed to what they want?"

"Exactly!"

Mase couldn't hold back a grin. As CEO of Chandler Industries, he'd heard far more sophisticated market analyses in his time, but none that cut to the heart of the matter as precisely as Chloe's onesies and twosies.

She chewed on her lower lip, obviously not as impressed with her marketing insights as Mase.

"I just wish I had a better customer base to work with. I mean, I'm not sure what percentage of the population I'm going to reach with this survey…or even what the population is around here."

"That's easy enough to find out. The government dumps all the data it collects in the census every ten years into computers."

"That's great for the government, but how does it help me?"

"You can request information on the population of any given area, sorted by city or township or county or Indian reservation or land grant or whatever. The data includes not just the number of people, but also the total number of housing units, average household income, number in the labor force, how much rent they pay…just about anything a business owner might want to know about her customer base."

"No kidding!"

Her violet eyes sparkled as she mulled over the possible uses for that kind of information. No doubt about it, Chloe Fortune was her father's daughter.

Even tucked away in a town with fewer residents than Emmet Fortune's well-staffed estate, the same fire to succeed burned in her as in her father and brother, Mac.

Mase was only too happy to feed that fire. If he hadn't already believed in her talents, the marketing strategy she'd outlined for the new Chandler Industries prototype jet in exchange for Mase's agreement to act as her pseudo-fiancé would have convinced him.

"The State Tourist Bureau could give you statistics on the transient population," he told her, fanning the flames. "Or the Parks and Recreation Division. You'll be amazed at the consumer information that's available if you know where to look for it."

She tilted her head back, studying him with those remarkable eyes. "You sound like a man who's looked for it."

"I have."

"What do you do, Mase? Back in Minneapolis?"

"I own a company that manufactures small aircraft. We sell primarily to the military, although a number of ranchers around these parts are flying Jetstars. Maybe you've flown in one of our planes?"

She had. Frequently. The last time was only a month ago, when Mase had piloted them on a visit to her cousin's ranch in Wyoming. He held his breath, waiting for a flicker of awareness.

Instead, the bright sparkle in her eyes dimmed by noticeable degrees. He caught confusion, despair, even a hint of panic, but no awareness.

"Maybe...maybe I have."

Cursing himself for pushing her, Mase tried to recover. "I have a friend who works for the government. Do you want me to make a call and get that data for you?"

"I...well—" She pulled herself together with an effort that hurt him to watch. "I'm not sure what I'll do with all that information, but, yes. Thank you."

"No problem. I'll help you sort through it. How about tonight, over dinner?"

Startled out of her moment of near panic, she blinked up at him. "You can get all that information by dinner?"

"Sure, I'll have it faxed in." He stopped, struck by a sudden thought. "There *is* a fax machine in Crockett, isn't there?"

"I'm not sure. I'll have to ask Hannah."

Chloe returned a few moments later with a crease in her brow. "Mayor Dobbins has the town's only fax machine."

"Is that a problem?"

"No, not really."

"Chloe?"

Sighing, she palmed her feathery bangs off her forehead. "Hannah's feeling...rambunctious today.

She says I'm welcome to do all the surveys and read all the census reports I want, but not to bother her with them. Not until I've made sense out of them, anyway."

"We'll make sense out of them," Mase assured her. "Over dinner. The mayor says he puts together a mean hamburger-and-home-fry combo. I'll bring enough for all of us."

After placing the order for dinner and obtaining the fax number from the helpful taxidermist cum mayor, Mase made a call to Pam Hawkins from the privacy of his room. He could almost hear the questions forming as he outlined his request. Pam had operated in the shadowy underworld too long to accept anything at face value. Sure enough, she churned out the questions as soon as he finished.

"Why do you need census data? And Parks and Recreation information, for heaven's sake? What's going on, Mase?"

"Nothing."

"Don't give me that crap. I know you. You're up to something. Come on, tell Pam. What are you going to do with this data?"

"All right, all right! If you must know, I'm going to use it to court my fiancée."

"Come again?"

"It's too complicated to explain now."

And too intensely private. Mase still hadn't adjusted to the kick in the gut he got every time Chloe looked at him with the polite friendliness of a stranger. Or to the idea that he'd have to win her trust…and her love…all over again.

"Just fax me the data this afternoon, will you? Any further sightings of our friend, Dexter Greene?"

As he'd known it would, the question instantly diverted Pam from the personal to the professional.

"No, not yet. We bugged your office and home phones, per your instructions, on the off-chance he'll try to get information of your whereabouts from someone on your staff."

"Keep me posted."

"I will."

"Mase…"

"Yeah?"

Uncharacteristically, Pam seemed to hesitate. Then her husky contralto rippled into laughter.

"You're the only man I know who'd woo a woman with Census Bureau data. Good luck."

"Thanks! I'll need it."

Six

Mase needed more than luck.

Courting Chloe, he soon discovered, required patience, pursuit and dogged persistence. It took him several days to develop and implement a strategy that worked. Not only did he have to take into consideration the long hours Chloe put in at the store and her refusal to leave Hannah alone. He also had to work around the competition. Every unattached male between the ages of nine and ninety seemed to have the same goal Mase did.

Shamelessly he played his insider's advantage to edge the locals out of the picture. He knew Chloe. Even more, he knew the stock she'd sprung from.

Fortune blood ran in her veins, and with it the business acumen that had vaulted the Fortune family business into an international conglomerate. Bit by bit Mase fanned the spark of her entrepreneurial instincts.

At his suggestion, she followed up her customer survey with a price comparison of the main staples stocked in the store. Calls to supermarkets and convenience stores in Custer, Hot Springs and Rapid City revealed that Hannah considerably underpriced many of the items she sold. Late Saturday evening, Chloe mulled over the results with Mase, her forehead creased.

"No wonder Hannah's having trouble paying her suppliers," she muttered. She caught herself and flushed. "Forget I said that. I shouldn't be talking about her business with outsiders."

The "outsiders" bit stung, but Mase let it pass. "Maybe the information you're gathering will convince her to raise her prices."

"I doubt it. Hannah's regulars are all her friends."

"This is her livelihood," he reminded her gently. "If you can show her ways to increase her profit margin without gouging her friends or driving away her customers, you'll be doing her a service."

"You're right. I know you're right." She let her gaze drift around the crowded store. "I just hope she doesn't think I'm meddling too much, or sticking my nose in where she doesn't want it.''

"If you are,'' he drawled, ''she'll let you know.''

Chloe's frown eased. ''Yes, she will.''

Hannah grumbled and harrumphed and said she had to study the figures before rushin' into any decisions. To Mase's secret amusement, Chloe interpreted that as a green light to go ahead with a top-to-bottom inventory of goods on hand. The following Tuesday she ruthlessly dragooned him and any of her admirers who wandered into the store into counting cans and cartons and rolls of tarred roofing paper.

"I've been wanting to do this since the first day I walked in the store,'' she confided, swiping her arm across a forehead streaked with dust. ''I don't think Hannah's inventoried her stock since... since...''

"Since the forties?'' Mase supplied.

His eyes dancing, he displayed a World War II ad for Chesterfield cigarettes he'd found stashed behind the cat food. He had to admit the variety and sheer number of items that showed up on the inventory amazed him as much as it did Chloe and her helpers.

"We carry six different flavors of oatmeal?'' she exclaimed a few minutes later, poring over the results as her helpers compiled them. "I didn't know there *were* six different flavors."

"Honeynut raisin's my favorite," one of the extras put in earnestly. "Hannah's store is about the only place that stocks it anymore."

"Hmm."

Mase hid a grin. His fiancée had not only taken to operating the Crockett General Store with as much proprietary interest as its owner, she was even beginning to sound like her.

The noncommittal response spooked her volunteer, a retired postal worker who'd gravitated to Crockett to indulge his passion for trout fishing. His fleshy jowls quivering, Charlie Thomas eyed Chloe uneasily.

"You're not thinking about cutting out the honeynut raisin, are you?"

She gave a small sigh. "It's not my place to cut out anything, Charlie. I'm just gathering information for Hannah to assess her stock."

"Okay," he muttered, "as long as she doesn't assess out my honeynut raisin."

Catching her lower lip in her teeth, Chloe sent Mase a glance that carried equal measures of resignation and laughter. The resignation made him grin. The laughter had him sucking in his breath. For a few heartbeats, the barriers between them came down. He saw his Chloe in the sparkling violet eyes, the smile that fought to break loose, even in the dust-streaked face and blond mane caught back in a plastic clip. The need to kiss her hollowed his stomach. He leaned forward an inch…two.

The laughter left her eyes. She stared at him for an instant…two. Then she blinked, and the barriers fell into place once again.

"We'd better get back to work," she said, gathering up her inventory lists.

To Mase's intense satisfaction, she sounded more than a little breathless. Good! Breathless constituted a considerable improvement over the distant politeness she'd treated him to at first. Maybe, just maybe, she was starting to trust him. Humming to himself, he went back to counting cans and plotting ways to take Chloe from breathless to panting.

Unintentionally, Hannah aided him in that effort the very next evening.

"No more, girl! No more of these dad-blamed facts and figures!"

With a grunt that tried to disguise her pain, the older woman shifted the cast encasing her leg from foot to mid-calf. Chagrined, Chloe closed the notebook she'd appropriated to tab and file her various reports.

"I'm sorry, Hannah. I didn't mean to pester you when you're hurting."

"It's the cold," her employer grumbled, trying to

get comfortable. "When the sun goes down, the damned pins in my ankle pick up the cold."

"Why don't I turn on the furnace?"

"I never fire it up until the fifteenth of October," her employer snapped. "Besides, I'm waiting on my delivery of fuel oil."

Which wouldn't occur until she paid the bill Chloe had found stuffed in a drawer, along with the overdue notices from several of her suppliers. Making a mental note to take care of the fuel bill herself from the wages Hannah had paid her, Chloe rose.

"I'll get you another blanket."

"I don't need another blanket. Stop fussing over me!"

The whiplike order stopped Chloe before she'd taken a single step. "I'm sorry."

Hannah took in her stricken expression and heaved a long sigh. "No, girl, I'm the one who's sorry. Truly. I guess I'm just feeling caged and takin' it out on you."

"You don't have to apologize. I know how difficult it is to…to operate at less-than-maximum capacity."

"Now that makes me feel even sorrier. You're handling your affliction a damn sight better than I am, Chloe."

"You're in a lot of pain."

"No, don't try to peel off my rough bark. I've been acting meaner than a she-wolf separated from the pack, snappin' your head off and grumblin' about your reports when you're just trying to help.''

Frowning, Hannah hitched up the blankets and tucked them under her armpits. ''Here, give me that notebook. And you, you get yourself out for a while. Take a walk. Go on down to the café for a bowl of chili. Shoot some pool.'' Her watery blue eyes grew sharper. ''Maybe take a ride with that Chandler fellow. He's been hanging around the store even more than Doc Johnson or that fool postman, Charlie Thomas, the past few days.''

''I know.''

''Chandler's got more in mind than just helpin' you count cans, girl.''

''I know.''

''Does that scare you?''

Chloe thought long and hard before answering. The thought of climbing into Mase's mud-splashed Blazer for a ride in the moonlight caused a distinct flutter deep in her belly, but the sensation had nothing to do with fear.

''No, it doesn't scare me.''

''Hmm.'' Hannah settled back against the cushions. ''Go on, get yourself out of here and let me try to make sense of all this gobbledygook. I've got the phone close to hand,'' she added irritably when Chloe hesitated. ''I'll call down to the café if I need anything.''

''Shall I bring you back some dinner?''

"No, no! I'm feelin' ornery, not hungry. You just scat."

The cold Hannah had complained about hit Chloe the moment she stepped outside. Thankfully, she'd taken the precaution of bundling up in one of the bright orange hunter's jackets Hannah stocked. Its downy fill toasted her from neck to mid-thigh, but the tip of her nose tingled in the sharp evening air.

The bright October sun still warmed the days, but the coming winter nipped at the night. Shoving her hands in her pockets, Chloe made her way slowly down the town's one main street. The passage of the season unsettled her far more than she'd admitted to Hannah.

Would she spend the winter here in Crockett? Would she spend forever in Crockett?

If not here, then where?

And with whom?

Unbidden, Mase's image crept into her mind. Chloe might have lost her memory, but she hadn't lost her wits. If Mase Chandler had come to Crockett to fish and hunt, he certainly hadn't made much use of the licenses she'd sold him. In the past few days he'd spent as much time at the store as he had roaming the hills around Crockett. What's more, he didn't even try to disguise the fact that he was attracted to her. She caught it in his glance, in the smile he reserved for her alone, in the careful restraint he'd exercised around her since that one, explosive kiss.

Was he staying in Crockett because of her? Had he come here in the first place because of her? Was there more between them than mere attraction?

Part of her wanted to believe there was.

Part of her didn't want to know there wasn't.

With that confused thought rattling around in her mind, she passed under the shaggy moose head mounted above the entrance to the café. Inside, the heavenly scent of sizzling meat and the equally heavenly sounds of a Mariah Carey ballad greeted her. She'd just started for the lunch counter when a heavy boot tread sounded on the stairs. She glanced up as Mase ducked under a low ceiling beam and appeared on the landing.

His black hair gleamed—from the shower, Chloe surmised. His jaw had that tinge of red that came with a recent shave. A blue wool sweater covered those world-class shoulders and softened the slate of his eyes to a bluish gray.

When he smiled down at her, intense pleasure pinwheeled through Chloe. She gulped, and decided she'd better get some answers to the questions she'd just asked herself before this searing pleasure led to something else, something she wasn't ready for.

"Your nose is pink," he said by way of greeting.

"It's cold out."

He flicked a quick glance at the darkened windows beside the door. "You shouldn't have walked down here alone. I would've picked you up or brought whatever you and Hannah wanted to the store."

"We've already imposed on you far more than we should have in the past few days." She hesitated, then began a subtle probe. "Before you know it, your vacation will be over and you'll have to head back to Minneapolis without racking up any real fishing or hunting time."

"I'm spending my time in Crockett just the way I want to."

That told her everything...and nothing. Obviously, subtle wouldn't work. "How long are you planning to stay here?"

"I haven't decided," he replied with a shrug before neatly turning the tables. "What about you? How long are you going to stay here?"

"I...I haven't decided."

For a moment Mase appeared ready to do some probing of his own. His eyes searched hers. A muscle ticked at the side of his jaw. Wanting answers from him, not questions, she preempted whatever he would have said by the simple expedient of shrugging out of her jacket and heading for the dining area.

"Hannah shooed me out of the store for a while. I was starting to get on her nerves, big-time. I decided to come down and see what Mayor Dobbins's special is tonight.''

"Do you want me to go up to the store and sit with Hannah while you're here?''

The offer melted an iceberg-size chunk of Chloe's reserve. Her smile shot up in both warmth and wattage.

"She has the phone close at hand and promised to call down here if she needed anything. Thanks for offering, though.''

"Anytime, Chloe.''

The way his voice dropped when he said her name tickled her ear. The low, rippling familiarity wasn't quite a caress, but it came close enough to start her nerve endings dancing under her skin. She could have sworn she'd heard that same tenderness, that same familiarity before.

"Mase…''

"Hey, Chloe!''

Harold Dobbins's cheerful greeting cut through the pounding in her heart. Biting back a sigh, Chloe turned and wove her way through the half dozen tables.

"Hello, Mr. Mayor.''

He chuckled. "That title sounds a whole lot more impressive than it really is.''

One of the ranch hands clicking pool balls on the felt-covered table at the back of the café snorted. "No kidding!''

"The Tuesday-night special is rib-eye, fresh off the hoof," the mayor announced, ignoring the cowboy's jibe. "I've got a couple of juicy steaks all ready to slap on the grill."

While Chloe was still trying to banish the image of her dinner on the hoof, Mase answered for them both. "Slap away."

"How do you like them cooked?"

"Make mine rare. Chloe likes hers medium well."

Her breath caught. She threw him a startled glance. "How did you know that?"

After a pause so brief she might have imagined it, he shrugged. "You wanted your hamburgers medium well the other night. Don't you like your steak the same way?"

"Oh." Her heart resumed its normal beat. "Right."

"Would you like a beer while we wait for dinner?"

"Sure."

While Mase got the drinks, Chloe chose a table. The café only boasted a half dozen or so, most of which were occupied by patrons hunched over platters of steak and fried potatoes swimming in thick white gravy. The Tuesday-night special had drawn a considerable crowd for Crockett.

Several patrons greeted her by name, others with a nod. To her surprise, a good number greeted Mase with the same casual friendliness. He'd certainly gotten to know folks in the…what?…four days he'd been in town.

Four days, she mused. It seemed longer. A lot longer. Frowning, Chloe hooked her jacket over the chair and studied Mase as he carried two dew-streaked bottles and two glasses to their table.

Okay. All right. She was attracted to him. That was understandable, given his rugged good looks and easy charm. She was also starting to like him. *Really* like him. But she couldn't quite bring herself to trust him. Not until she got answers to the questions whirling around in her head.

Unfortunately, she didn't get any during dinner. As she'd learned in the past few weeks, the residents of Crockett were a gregarious lot. Most of them, anyway. One loner with scraggly gray hair kept his shoulders hunched over his dinner and his fork working, but the rest of the café's patrons carried on conversations that flowed across tables.

Inevitably, they drew Chloe and Mase into lively discussions of the weather, the price of beef and the governor's chances in the upcoming November elections. The mayor dished up gory details about the first day of elk season that Chloe could have done without, along with huge platters of steak and home fries. When Mase finally pushed his plate away, groaning, the winner of the pool game sauntered over. Seeking a new victim, he tossed out a challenge.

"Go ahead," Chloe said with a smile. "I'll watch."

Watch she did. Perched on a tall stool safely out of the range of the cue sticks, she was in perfect position to take in the bantering rivalry and the clack of the pool balls, not to mention the long, tight lines of Mase's body when he leaned over the table to make a shot. By the end of the first game, her throat was dry. By the end of the second, her heart thumped against her ribs. When they racked up the third and final set, she could barely hear the jukebox over the pounding in her ears.

Even then, she wasn't ready for the dart of pure delight she experienced when Mase laughed and paid the jubilant victor three dollars. Or for the sudden catch in her throat when he turned and held out his hand.

"I'm better at dancing than pool. Barely. Would you like to work off some of that steak?"

Chloe swallowed. She wanted answers, didn't she? What better way to get them than to slide off the stool and into Mase's arms? If there was more between them than just this simmering attraction, this tug of sensual need, surely she'd feel it. Slowly she put her hand in his.

The pool table took up most of the dance floor. The old Mac Davis tune pouring out of the jukebox called for more of a two-step than the waltz Mase pulled her into. Chloe didn't sweat the minor details. As she fit herself to his long length, her entire being focused on the sensations that registered on her whirling mind. The leathery-lemon tang of his aftershave. The play of his muscles under her fingertips. The press of her hips against his. The way her temple brushed his chin.

Each sensation heightened her awareness of the man who held her. Every move, every breath added to the sexual desire spinning out of control. Yet it wasn't until the song ended and they were walking off the tiny dance floor that Chloe plunged from desire into shock.

Mase put his hand at the small of her back to guide her to the table. His touch was light, the gesture courteous...and electrifying!

The instant she felt the press of his fingers, Chloe stopped in her tracks. Her spine tingled. Shivers raced through her whole body. After the intimacy of the dance, she didn't know why this casual contact should stun her, but it did. It also kicked the door that had closed in her mind open another few inches. The haze clouding her mind swirled, shifted, settled.

He'd touched her like this before! She was sure of it! With this same careful control. This same deliberate casualness.

"Chloe?"

Mase's deep voice spun her around. Her breath

came fast and hard. She stared up at him, willing the mists to part just a little more. When they didn't, she gave a groan of sheer frustration.

"Chloe, what is it? Are you all right?"

She brushed aside his sharp concern. She had to know, had to understand what had just happened.

"You're staying here, aren't you?"

His eyes narrowed. "I have a room upstairs."

"Take me upstairs."

His hesitation stretched almost to infinity. Finally he shook his head. "I don't think that's a good idea."

"Why not?"

"If I take you upstairs, I'm not promising I'll keep my hands off you."

The growled warning sent shock spilling through her. Shock, and a hot, sweet desire that prickled her skin from her nose to her knees.

"I...I need to talk to you," she gasped. "Just talk."

"I'm still not making any promises. I want you, Chloe. I have for a long time."

How long? she wondered wildly. Days? Weeks? Years? Oh, God, why couldn't she remember? Why couldn't she kick that damned door all the way open?

She would, she vowed fiercely. She would!

"All right. Maybe going up to your room isn't such a good idea. Why don't you go back to the store with me? We can talk there."

Seven

Calling himself ten kinds of a fool for not sweeping Chloe up the stairs and into his bed, Mase growled his assent.

"All right. I'll tell Mayor Dobbins to throw another rib-eye on for Hannah, then we'll go up to the store."

"She doesn't want anything. As she put it, she's feeling too pesky to eat."

"Fine. Get your coat while I settle the bill."

"I'll pay for my din—"

"Get your coat."

The whiplike command brought her chin up. "I'll pay for my dinner, Chandler. Yours, too, as a belated thank-you for helping me with the customer database and the inventory.''

The militant glint in her eyes warned Mase not to argue further. Muttering a curse, he dragged a hand through his hair and accepted her offer with something less than graciousness.

''I'll wait for you outside.''

He strode to the exit, battling the heat that had seared him when he'd held her during that dance...and the even fiercer fire that had leaped into his belly when she'd invited herself upstairs. He had to douse those fires, had to cool off before he spooked her or, worse, sent her retreating even further behind the barriers.

The cold night air helped considerably. So did the long strides he took up and down the street. By the time Chloe emerged from the café, he'd regained at least an outward semblance of control.

They made the short ride to the store in silence. The bell tinkled as they stepped into its fragrant warmth. A quick sweep of the store showed it empty of customers and, thank goodness, any and all lovesick vets or postal workers or ranch hands.

Shedding her bright orange jacket, Chloe headed for the back room. ''I'll check on Hannah. Make yourself comfortable.''

Right. Comfortable.

Mase ignored the rocking chairs pulled up to the potbellied stove and prowled the few feet of open space in front of the counter. After his crack about wanting her, she was going to want answers. He'd better come up with some, fast.

He paced, framing his responses. The floorboards creaked under his boots. Muffled voices carried from the distant living quarters. Mase catalogued Hannah's gruff tones. The note of polite inquiry in Chloe's. Another feminine voice he didn't recognize.

Although…

He stopped, frowning, as the voice tugged at his mind. Before he could place it, Chloe returned.

"Does Hannah have company?"

"An old friend stopped by."

"Anyone you know?"

Her shimmering violet eyes darkened. "No."

The single syllable carried an aching frustration that cut through Mase like a jagged blade. He braced himself, guessing that the worst was yet to come.

He was right.

Dragging in a deep breath, Chloe plunged right to the heart of the matter. "I felt something, back there at the café. When we were walking to the table and you put your hand on my back, I had the oddest sense that you'd done it before. Many times. You have, haven't you?"

"Yes."

"Who are you? How did we know each other?"

The tendons in Mase's neck corded. He'd waited

for this moment for days. Slowly, carefully, he closed the distance between them.

"I'm your fiancé."

"We…we were engaged?"

His jaw worked. "We're still engaged."

"But how…? Why…?"

She stumbled to a stop. Mase's heart jackhammered against his ribs. The hands fisted at his sides felt clammy. Don't push her, he warned himself savagely. Let her take one step at a time. One question at a time.

Finally she sorted through the thousands that had to be tumbling through her mind and cut to the core.

"Who am I?"

"Your name is Chloe Fortune."

"Chloe Fortune."

She tested the name, repeating it again, then again. Taut as strung wire, Mase waited for a flicker of recognition, of awareness, of relief. All he saw in her face was a bleak despair that tore at his soul.

"Do I…" She fought for each strangled word. "Do I have a family?"

"You have a father and two brothers. Plus several dozen assorted aunts, uncles and cousins back in Minneapolis."

"Minneapolis? Is that where I…where we lived?"

Mase had never really believed the old cliché about a heart breaking. The brutal knowledge that

Chloe didn't remember anything of her former life...or of him...was fast making a believer out of him.

Mindful of the neurologist's advice, he gritted his teeth and waited for her to take the next step. At the least, he expected her to demand details of her family and her former life. At the worst, he feared she'd allow the panic he saw in her face drive her further back into the shadows.

She did neither. Instead, she closed her eyes. Breathing hard, she battled her panic with a raw courage that made Mase's chest ache. When she opened them again, he had to forcibly restrain himself from reaching for her.

"Do you recall anything from before you arrived in Crockett?" he asked gently.

"I remember a long, dark stretch of road. I remember flashes of an accident. I remember going to a doctor." She lifted a trembling hand to rub her temple. "Sometimes..."

His pulse jumped. "Sometimes?"

"Sometimes I almost remember why I was on that road."

Mase wanted to tell her. He had the story all ready. But the delicate balance of truth and fiction he'd created to explain the scene she'd witnessed in his office stuck in his throat. He couldn't lie to her. Not now. Not when she was so exposed and vulnerable.

"I feel as though a door has closed on my mind," she admitted, her voice raw with frustration. "The damned thing opens an inch or two, then slams shut.

"It'll open the rest of the way, Chloe. Give yourself time."

To his astonishment, she managed a ragged chuckle. "That's what Hannah says. South Dakota may be knee-deep in snow before I finally kick it all the way open."

"It doesn't matter how deep the snow is," he told her. "I came to Crockett to take you home. I'm staying right here until you're ready to make the journey."

The soft promise brought her hand down and her head up. "I'm not ready yet, Mase. I don't want to go home until I know why I ran away from it. And from you."

Mase was still digesting that when she rocked him back on his heels. Reaching up, she framed his face with her palms.

"I do know one thing, though. I wasn't running from this." Stretching up on tiptoe, she brushed her lips across his.

"Chloe…"

"Or this."

Tilting her head, she fitted her mouth to his. Mase let her taste. Touch. Test. All the while his fists were clenched so tight he thought his knuckles would pop.

"I didn't run away from this," she murmured against his mouth. "Did I, Mase? Did I?"

Chloe had her answer even before he growled a negative and slid a hand in her hair to anchor her head for the kiss she demanded. Whatever else had driven her away, it wasn't the hard crush of Mase Chandler's mouth on hers. Or the flex of his muscles as he wrapped an arm around her waist and drew her into his heat. His strength didn't cage her. His hunger didn't frighten her.

If anything, it fed her own.

Determined to crack the door open another inch or two, she wrapped her arms around his neck. Her mouth ground into his. Her breasts flattened against his chest. He matched her, move for move, his legs widening, his hand burrowing deeper into her hair. She felt him harden against her hip, felt the wild slam of his heart against hers.

Without quite knowing when or how it happened, Chloe lost control of the kiss and of the situation. Her senses rocketed toward maximum overload. She breathed Mase, tasted him, touched him at every contact point from knee to nose. Her blood pounded so hard and so fast that she barely heard the tap of footsteps behind her.

Mase heard them, though. His body wire tight, he lifted his head.

"Excuse me," a feminine voice offered in apology. "I didn't mean to disturb you."

Dragging in great gulps of air and regret, Chloe stepped out of his arms. With one hand on the counter to steady herself, she turned to Hannah's friend. Taller and more willowy than the shopkeeper, the woman wore scuffed boots, well-washed jeans, a bulky sheepskin vest and a narrow-brimmed felt hat pulled low on her forehead. On most of the ranchers in the area, the outfit looked functional. On her, it looked elegant.

"You're not disturbing us." The monumental lie almost choked Chloe. "Did you, uh, want something?"

With a look that combined lively interest and intense speculation, she shook her head. "No, not really. Hannah was feeling a little fretful, so I thought I'd better leave. You two just go back to what you were doing."

She strode toward the door, her boots ringing on the boards. Mase watched the older woman until the door closed. When he turned back to Chloe, she saw her own frustration reflected in his eyes.

The interruption had come just in time for both of them, Chloe knew. Another few moments and she would have been yanking at the buttons on his shirt or grabbing for his belt buckle. She needed to back off, now! She needed to let the heat still scorching her skin cool. She needed to digest what Mase had told her and decide what questions she wanted answers for next.

Knowing what she needed to do was a whole lot easier than doing it, however. Her throat aching, she tried for a smile.

"I'd better go help Hannah get ready for bed."

He nodded.

"Can we continue this…this discussion tomorrow? I want to know more, Mase. About us. About my family. I'll get someone to stay with Hannah tomorrow afternoon. Maybe we could go for a walk or drive up to the lake."

He lifted a hand and brushed the back of it down her cheek. "After tonight, I don't guarantee you'll be any safer at the lake than in the privacy of my room, Chloe."

She swiped her tongue along suddenly dry lips. "I'll take my chances."

Fierce satisfaction leaped into his face. He kissed her again, hard and long, then left her with a promise.

"Tomorrow afternoon."

The bell above the door jangled as he left. Before the last echoes died away, Chloe was already regretting his departure.

As Mase had expected, the pseudo-rancher was waiting for him outside the store. Boots crossed at the ankle, hands tucked in the pockets of her sheepskin vest, she leaned against the cab of a pickup.

Her breath steamed on the chill night air. Under the brim of her low-riding hat, her face was shadowed.

"Hello, Kate."

Kate Fortune's rich chuckle drifted on the night air. "Hello, Mase. For a moment there, I wasn't sure you'd recognized me."

"For a moment there, I didn't."

The laughter faded from her voice. "Chloe certainly didn't. I was devastated when she walked in and gave me the same polite nod she'd give a stranger."

"I've been on the receiving end of a few of those polite nods myself this past week."

"Is that right?" She lifted an eyebrow. "It looked like you were on the receiving end of more than that a few moments ago."

"We're making progress," he replied with some understatement.

"Maybe if you'd made that kind of progress during your engagement," Kate tossed back tartly, "my great-niece wouldn't have run away."

Mase grimaced. "I've been telling myself the same thing."

Kate pushed away from the truck. Her face, still unlined and beautifully boned, wore a troubled frown. Reaching out, she clasped both of his hands in hers.

"How is she, Mase? Really?"

His fingers curled over hers. In the years Mase

had known Chloe's great-aunt, he'd come to respect her for her business acumen. He'd also shaken his head in awe at her more remarkable exploits, admired her thoroughbred beauty and cherished her for the love she lavished on her sprawling family.

"I think she's starting to recover, Kate. Memories are tugging at her, although she can't seem to pull them out of the haze in her mind yet."

"Emmet will be glad to hear that! He's stewing himself into an early grave over Chloe's long absence."

"I've been giving him nightly progress reports. He didn't tell me you were coming out to South Dakota."

"He didn't know," Kate replied with a twinkle. "I don't coordinate my activities with my sons or nephews, only with Sterling...and then I usually wait until it's too late for him to protest."

Mase hid a grin. Long-suffering Sterling Foster had loved Kate for years with all the passion of his quiet, conservative, Ivy-league heart. Only after Kate's supposed death in a plane crash and the stealthy investigation to find her killer, had the attorney come out and declared his love.

Theirs was, the Fortunes all declared, the perfect match. Stodgy, steady Sterling and beautiful, adventurous Kate. One soared with the eagles. The other gave her the stable platform she needed to take off from.

Not unlike his match with Chloe, Mase reflected wryly. In the eyes of the Fortunes, he was the solid, steady and reliable one in their relationship. Only his fiancée had gained a fleeting glimpse into his other life…a glimpse they were both paying for now.

"I'd better get back to Rapid City," Kate said a few moments later. "I left the crew standing by at the plane."

Mase opened the door to the pickup for her, then leaned down to catch her soft question. "When are you two coming home?"

"Whenever Chloe's ready."

Sighing, Kate nodded.

Hands shoved deep in his pockets, Mase watched the pickup's taillights bounce down Crockett's main street before disappearing at the turnoff for the state road.

Strange. He'd arrived in town less than a week ago, determined to reclaim his fiancée and take her back to Minneapolis. He still wanted to reclaim Chloe. His hunger for her mounted every day and had come close to bursting its bounds tonight. But she was a different person here. He was different. Stripped of their past by Chloe's amnesia, they were getting to know each other all over again. Discovering their likes and dislikes. Peeling away the complications engendered by their phony engagement.

And tomorrow, Mase thought with a sudden lurch

in his stomach, they'd peel away more than complications. The mere thought of a few hours alone with Chloe had him hard again. Grimacing at the now-familiar ache in his groin, he climbed into the Blazer. The cold night air whipped through his opened window as he drove the short distance to the café/hotel/town offices.

Tomorrow, he promised the stars and himself. Tomorrow.

Tomorrow, Chloe thought as she helped Hannah get settled for the night. Tomorrow.

She'd learn more about herself. About her family. About Mase. She'd touch him again. Taste him. Anticipation curled her toes. A hunger she didn't even try to deny licked at her veins.

It was still with her when she went back to close up the store. With brisk efficiency, she emptied the cash drawer and tallied the receipts in the log Hannah kept for that purpose. Rubber-banding the receipts to the log, she set them aside to take to Hannah and went to turn out the porch lights and lock the front door.

She'd just reached for the latch when a face suddenly loomed in the glass. Her heart almost jumped out of her chest. Gasping, she jerked back.

The stranger on the other side of the glass peered at her for a moment, then reached for the door latch. The bell jangled discordantly as he stepped inside.

"Evening, ma'am." He tipped two fingers to the ball cap that covered his scraggly gray hair. "Sorry if I startled you."

Chloe stared at him. Ripples of excitement darted down her spine. She knew him! She knew him from somewhere! Maybe the blasted door blocking her mind had finally started to swing open.

Almost immediately, she recognized him as the solitary diner from the café. Her excitement fluttered into intense disappointment. Masking it with some effort, she pinned a smile on her face.

"Can I help you?"

"Yes, ma'am. I'm out of cigarette makings. Could you point me to them?"

"They're on the shelf over there, by the beer."

"Thank you."

While he searched among the varieties of papers and tobacco for his favorite brands, Chloe went back behind the counter. A few moments later he dropped his choices on the wood surface and gave her the yellow-toothed smile of a heavy smoker.

"Didn't I see you down at the café a while ago?" he asked while she rang up the sale.

"Yes, you did."

"With your young fellow?"

"He's not really— Well, he's…"

She searched for the right words to describe her feelings for the man she'd just kissed. With a sense of the inevitable, she finally admitted the truth.

"I guess that description fits Mase as well as anything else."

Her customer pocketed his change and his purchases. "That's his name? Mase? Don't think I've ever heard that name 'round these parts."

"He's not from around here." Anxious to finish closing and curl up with her still-whirling emotions, Chloe rounded the end of the counter. "If you don't need anything else, I'll lock up as you leave."

His lips pulled back over his stained teeth.

"No, thank you, ma'am. I don't need anything else. I got what I came for."

For the life of her, Chloe couldn't say why that smile made her uneasy. The man spoke and acted politely enough. His slacks and plaid shirt had seen a few washings, but they were clean and neat, as were his sturdy work boots.

Maybe it was the gleam in his brown eyes. Or those yellowed teeth that gave him an almost wolfish appearance. Whatever the reason for Chloe's prickle of unease, it disappeared when the lock snicked into place behind her late customer.

She dismissed it, and him, and went about the small tasks associated with closing up the Crockett General Store. The beer sign above the cooler clicked off. The floorboards creaked as she checked the windows. Metal clanged against metal when she used the poker to break apart the glowing ash in the potbellied stove.

The now-familiar routine occupied only a small part of her conscious thought. An *un*familiar, steadily mounting anticipation occupied the rest.

Tomorrow, Chloe thought, her heart thumping as she switched off the lights and plunged the store into darkness.

Tomorrow.

Eight

"**T**hanks so much for volunteering to stay with Hannah for a few hours, Charlie."

Chloe sent the retired postal worker a warm smile, which raised a flush on his fleshy face and a disgruntled harrumph from Hannah.

"The way you wet nurse me, girl, you'd think I had all of six years tucked under my belt instead of sixty and then some."

Chloe ignored her employer's grumbling. She barked often, but rarely bit.

"Really, Hannah, I don't mind," Charlie put in. "In fact, I wanted to talk to you about handheld scanners. I called my former boss at the post office.

He said we could get one of the older models at the next government surplus auction."

"What the devil do I want with a handheld scanner? That herd of buffalo over at Custer State Park will learn to fly before I learn how to use something like that."

"I'll help you," her visitor offered.

"You will?" Surprise, then understanding dawned on Hannah's sun-weathered face. "I've got your game, Charlie Thomas. You just want to spend more time sniffin' around Chloe, don't you?"

The postal worker flushed, but he answered with a simple dignity that tugged at both women's hearts.

"To tell the truth, trout fishing doesn't fill up as much of my time as I thought it would. I'd be happy to help out more at the store, if you'd let me."

"Hmmmm." Folding her arms across her chest, Hannah regarded him skeptically for long moments. "Tell me again about those handheld thingama-bobs."

Chloe took that grudging request as her exit cue. With a promise to return within a few hours, she hurried through the storeroom and snatched up a plastic cooler off the counter. The excitement she'd held at bay all morning sizzled and spit along her nerves as she stepped through the door and into the flood of noon sunshine.

Mase was waiting for her—all long, lithe male and lazy patience. A fanciful little breeze ruffled his black hair. He'd rolled up the sleeves of his blue denim shirt in concession to the unexpected October warmth. His jeans rode low on his lean waist. Arms folded across his broad chest, hips propped against the fender of the black-and-tan Blazer, eyes shielded by mirrored sunglasses, he looked as tough and as rugged as the granite mountains surrounding Crockett.

Her pulse skipped, skittered, then careened all over the place when he straightened, peeled off the sunglasses and reached for the cooler she'd brought with her.

"Here, let me take that." His brows lifted at its weight. "Good Lord, what did you pack in here?"

"Half the contents of the Crockett General Store. Hannah insisted that the air up at the lake would do a serious number on our appetites."

Actually, her employer had predicted that Chloe's bottom-hugging jeans and snug, long-sleeved turquoise top would do more for Mase's appetite than anything packed in the cooler. From the way his gray eyes roamed hungrily over her curves, the prediction appeared right on target.

Like mountain wildflowers unfurling their petals to the sun, Chloe's body responded to the hunger Mase didn't even try to disguise. Her heart fluttered. Her stomach tightened. Tiny pinpricks of sensation budded her nipples under the turquoise cotton. She had to fight for each breath as he opened the back of the Blazer and deposited the cooler amid a tangle of equipment.

"What's all that?" she asked.

"Rods and reels. I thought you might like to try your hand at casting a few flies. Unless," he added with a wicked grin, "you'd prefer to reach into the bait box and grab a dozen or so night crawlers."

"Not hardly."

"Are you sure? We could stretch out on the bank and just veg out while the worms do all the work."

"Worms or no worms, I fully intend to stretch out on the bank," Chloe informed him loftily. "I can't remember the last time I just vegged for a whole afternoon."

The irony of her words didn't strike her until Mase closed the passenger door. She couldn't remember a lot more than the last time she'd lazed in the sun. Staunchly, she refused to let panic and confusion creep over her. She wouldn't allow them to spoil her mood or dim the bright sunshine.

She had a name. Chloe Fortune. She had a father and two brothers in Minneapolis. She was engaged to the man who slid into the seat beside her...or so he claimed. That was enough to hold back the shadows. For now.

As if sensing her mood, Mase kept the conversation light and easy during the short drive up to the lake. Chloe put in an occasional comment, but for the most part she was content to simply breathe in the pine-scented air and absorb the rich baritone of his voice. Alternating patterns of light and dark played across his face as he wheeled the Blazer around hairpin turns studded on both sides by stands of tall, lodgepole pine. Fifteen minutes later he turned off the blacktop.

"Are you sure you know where you're going?" Chloe asked, bracing a hand against the dash as the vehicle jounced along a dirt track.

"I'm sure."

She eyed the narrow track doubtfully as it led them deeper into the forest. Sunlight struggled to knife through the canopy formed by thick stands of pine and curly barked aspens. Low-hanging boughs swished against the Blazer's roof. A squirrel scolded loudly as the vehicle passed too close to its nest.

Just when Chloe was wondering if the forest had swallowed them completely, she caught a glimpse of indigo amid the endless green. Seconds later the Blazer bounced out of the trees and rolled to a stop scant yards from the shore of a tiny, perfect lake.

"Oh!" Enchanted, Chloe climbed out of the vehicle. "Oh, Mase, it's beautiful!"

"I thought so, too," he replied with a touch of proprietary smugness, as if he was the first human to discover the lake's serene beauty.

Like polished glass, the water reflected the surrounding peaks and pines. Only upon closer examination did Chloe discover that it was as crystalline clear below the surface as it was above. She clambered atop one of the boulders that lined the shore and peered down at the rocks and pebbles on the bottom.

"It looks like I could reach right down and touch the bottom. How deep do you think it is?"

"Deep enough to wet you down if you fall in." Opening the Blazer's back hatch, Mase started to unload. "Do you want to eat first or try your hand at casting?"

"You're serious about this fishing business?"

"Absolutely. It's one of the purer pleasures in life."

"Not for the fish," Chloe retorted, scrambling off her boulder to help him unload. "Let's eat. I'm starved."

They spread the blanket Mase had shamelessly purloined from his room beside a huge boulder. A thick layer of pine needles provided a springy cushion under the blanket. While Mase lazed back against the boulder, resting an arm on a drawn-up knee, Chloe unpacked the cooler.

"Beer for you, wine spritzers for me."

"Sounds good."

"Sourdough rolls, sliced ham, roast beef and smoked turkey breast."

"Sounds even better."

"Cheddar, provolone and lemon-peppered brie."

"Lemon-peppered brie?" A grin tugged at one

corner of his mouth. "I bet you don't get a lot of demand for that at the Crockett General Store."

"No, we don't," she admitted, uncurling the foil wrapper. "But the distributor offered me some samples and I couldn't resist."

She dug in the cooler for the plates and plastic utensils, then spread a crust of roll with the soft, creamy cheese. "Here, try a bite. Tell me what you think."

Leaning forward, Mase took the morsel in his mouth. He also took the tips of Chloe's fingers. Startled, she felt the tender scrape of his teeth all the way from her wrist to her elbow. She jerked a little, but didn't pull her hand away.

"Mmmm." He leaned back, a gleam of satisfaction in his eyes. "Good. Very good. What else have you got?"

"What? Oh."

Recalled to her duties as hostess, she pulled out fruit, foil containers of baked beans and potato salad, pickles, mustard, mayonnaise and a giant-size bag of chocolate chip cookies. When she finished, the spread took up most of the blanket.

"We got enough here to feed six people," she said ruefully, eyeing the lavish display.

"If you're half as hungry as I am, we'll polish it off," Mase predicted confidently.

To her surprise, they did. Or a good portion of it, anyway. Lazy and replete, Chloe leaned back against the boulder while Mase performed cleanup duty. That done, he stretched out beside her and slid an arm around her shoulders to cushion her from the rock.

She had to admit he made an excellent cushion. Muscles smooth and warmed by the sun shifted to nest her comfortably against him. A faint hint of starch from his shirt mingled with the scent of aftershave and clean, healthy male. Chloe felt his heart beating strong and sure against her side.

For long, quiet moments, she savored the peace, the warmth, the sheer beauty of the placid lake. If only she could bottle this serenity and carry it around in her pocket to unstopper whenever the uncertainty and shadows started to close in on her.

She couldn't, of course, but she could do the next best thing—push the shadows away once and for all. Here, in the comfort of Mase's warmth, Chloe almost believed she could do just that.

"Tell me about my father."

"He's a good man," Mase said quietly. "One of the best. Your mother died of an embolism when you and your twin, Chad, were only a week old. Emmet and your older brother, Mac, raised the two of you with so much love that you once told me you never missed your mother."

Some of the brightness went out of the sun. How could she not remember a father and brother who loved her like that?

"What's he like? My father, I mean."

Mase smiled. "Big. Bluff. As blond as you until he went gray."

The description caused an ache in Chloe's chest. This was hard. Far harder than last night, when all she had to deal with were names. Now she struggled to visualize gray-streaked blond hair. A smile.

"And...and my brothers? How well do you know them?"

He caught the catch in her voice. His arm slid down to curl around her waist. In a tender, gentle move, he brought her into his lap.

"Mac—Mackenzie—and I went to school together. He was hell on wheels when he wanted to be, but he always took his family responsibilities seriously, even as a boy. He recently married. You now have a brand-new niece named Annie."

"Annie. Annie Fortune."

Oh, God! Why couldn't she remember Mac or his wife or little Annie? The tranquility of the lake seemed to shimmer, then slowly evaporate. A numbness spread through Chloe's chest as she listened while Mase gave her more names, descriptions, details.

When he paused, she swallowed to clear a throat growing tighter by the moment. "What about us? How did we meet? When did we get engaged?"

"I probably first saw you when you were still in diapers, but you didn't really make much of an impression until Mac brought you and Chad over to my folks' house one afternoon after school. You must have been about four or five then. You scarfed down a gallon and a half of rocky road ice cream, then threw up all over my sneakers."

"Charming."

His chuckle reverberated under her ear. "We saw each other off and on while you were growing up, and even dated a few times when you returned from Paris last year."

She angled her head back to stare up at him. "A few times? We got engaged after dating only a few times?"

Mase's stomach tightened. For a moment he was tempted to shade the truth. To take advantage of the confusion clouding Chloe's eyes and tell her that those casual dates plunged them headlong into passion, which in turn led to love.

A few weeks ago, even a few days ago, he might have done just that. He'd lived a life colored by deceptions and half-truths for so long, he was a master at making even the most dangerous lies seem real. He couldn't do that to Chloe now, though. He couldn't do it to himself.

"Our engagement started off as more of a business deal," he told her softly. "You worked up the marketing strategy for Chandler Industries' new twin-engine jet. In return, I agreed to run interference for you with your father.''

He thought she might ask about the marketing strategy, or why she needed him to run interference with her father. Instead, she picked up on a subtle inflection in his explanation.

''Our engagement *began* as a business deal? How…how was it supposed to end?''

Mase didn't have to think about an answer to that one. Smiling, he bent his head. ''Like this, sweetheart. Just like this.''

She tasted of strawberry spritzer and chocolate chip cookies and sweet, sweet Chloe. Mase savored each flavor, each swirl of delight. Her lips parted under his, and the sweetness grew richer, warmer, darker.

Then she was clinging to him, her arms tight, her mouth urgent with a need that started a slow, pulsing ache in his groin. When Chloe moaned softly and flattened herself against him, that slow ache vaulted straight into supercharged. Sweat pooled at the base of his spine. His arms trembled with the urge to tumble her back, to strip off her shirt and bare her to the sun and his mouth.

Mase fought the urge with everything in him. She had to set the pace, he reminded himself fiercely. He'd take no more than she wanted to give. Even with that savage warning, he wasn't ready for the emotion that hit him like a fist when she pulled back.

"Why don't I remember this?" she cried. "What if I never remember?"

The tears shimmering in her violet eyes destroyed what was left of Mase's control. He could no more have held back at that point than he could've stopped breathing.

"It doesn't matter." He speared his fingers through her hair and turned her face up to his. "We'll make a whole new set of memories. Enough to last a lifetime."

"But…"

"Right now. Right here. Like this, my darling. And this. And this."

Gasping, Chloe arched as he nipped at her lips, her throat, the slope of her breast. His mouth set off tiny explosions all through her body. His raw hunger raised an answering fervor. Her nails dug into his neck, holding him, encouraging him. Not that he needed encouragement. Her nipples peaked at his caress. Her belly tightened with each stroke, each kiss, each scrape of his teeth against the cotton shirt covering her skin.

It might have been mere moments or long hours before Chloe scrambled off his lap and up on her knees. Hip to hip, chest to chest, mouth to mouth, she ground against him, as if trying to anchor herself to the reality he represented.

"Mase. Please. I want you to love me. I need…I need you to love me."

"I do. I will."

Her fingers fumbled with his shirt buttons, wanting, needing the feel of his flesh against hers. She tugged the shirt down, glided her hands up his arms, dropped kisses everywhere her fingers touched. His skin was so warm, tasted so wonderful. Her tongue trailed across his collarbone, traced a puckered scar in his shoulder. She pulled back, hurting for his hurt.

"How did you get this? And this," she added, tracing the hard ridge of flesh on one rib with an unsteady fingertip.

"I guess I dodged when I should have ducked," he said with a grin, lowering his head to do a little tasting himself. His lips and his tongue worked such magic that Chloe soon forgot the scar, forgot the odd ridge of flesh across his rib, almost forgot to breathe.

They were both panting when he took her down to the blanket and slid a leg between hers. His knee slid higher and rode hard against her core. The exquisite torture sent shards of pleasure splintering through Chloe. His mouth and his hands all over her body heated those jagged shards to white-hot. She writhed under him, hungry and hurting and riddled with need.

Afterward, she could never recall whether she stripped off her shirt or Mase did. Whether he peeled down her jeans first, or she reached for his. All that mattered at the time was the driving imperative to join with him, to find herself in him.

She would! She'd find herself, and something more, someone more. She waited, almost sobbing with impatience while Mase dug in his jeans pocket for protection. The muscles in his back rippled. His black hair glistened with a faint sheen of sweat at the temples. Against the backdrop of the piercing blue sky, he looked magnificent, as strong and untamed as the mountains that surrounded them.

When he turned and smiled at her, Chloe's heart leaped. The door in her mind creaked open. Almost, she could see beyond it. Almost, she could hear the voices calling to her.

Then Mase fit himself between her thighs, lowered his weight onto his forearms, and proceeded to send every thought, every shadowy image into a never-never land of sweet, spiraling desire.

With a skill that left her breathless, he primed her. His teeth teased her breasts into aching, burning want. His hand cupped her mound, rubbing, stroking. When his fingers slid to the slick wetness between her legs, Chloe opened for him eagerly.

"I've wanted you for so long." Muscles taut, voice low and raw, he fit himself against her. "I've loved you for so long."

"Oh, Mase. I must have loved you, too. I couldn't feel the way I do now if I hadn't." She wrapped her arms around his neck, gasping as he filled her. "You...you were right. The past doesn't matter. Only this. Only now."

Her hips and her heart lifted as one. Joyfully, she drew him in. This was right. This was a memory, a moment she'd hold in her heart forever. Wherever they went from here, this was right.

He thrust slowly at first, then deeper, harder, faster. The rhythm was like a song—primitive and enduring and endless and perfect. Her neck arched. Her back bowed. The pleasure centered low in her belly, intensified, exploded. She cried out, riding the waves for what seemed like forever, until Mase drove into her a final time and crested with her.

He buried his face in her neck, shuddering. Eyes closed, body limp, Chloe clung to him. Haze still shrouded the edges of her mind, but she felt like a lone, lost sailor who'd somehow made it through mist-shrouded seas and sailed into home port.

That sense of slowly finding her way through the fog stayed with her during the incredible hour afterward, when she lay with her head on Mase's arm, her eyes closed and her face turned to the sun. The same feeling gathered even greater intensity when they made love again, more gently this time, more slowly.

But it wasn't until they drove back to Crockett and pulled up in front of the store that the mists parted, finally and irrevocably. Chloe climbed out of the Blazer, intending to help Mase unload the cooler and the remains of their lunch. When the bell above the door jangled, she threw an idle glance over her shoulder at the woman who pushed through the door and stepped onto the porch.

"It's about time you got back."

At the sound of her smoky contralto, Chloe's heart stuttered, then stopped. The blood drained from her face. Icy recognition poured through every cell in her body.

She knew that voice!

She knew this woman!

Numb, she watched the tall, elegant brunette hurry down the steps and head directly for Mase.

Nine

Hawkins. Pam Hawkins.

The name cut through the haze in Chloe's mind like a high-powered spotlight lasering through a midnight sky. Fragments of scenes came sweeping back to her. A sun-filled reception area. A paneled office. This sleek, sharp-featured woman laughing up at Mase while she played with his tie.

Shocked into immobility by the sudden rush of memories, Chloe stood unmoving as the brunette brushed past her in a cloud of expensive perfume.

''I've got to talk to you, Mase. Now!''

Her breath lodged halfway down her throat, Chloe waited for him to reply.

His face grim, Mase dropped the cooler back into the Blazer and went to meet the newcomer.

"What's going on?"

No hello, Chloe noted, dying a little inside. No exclamation of surprise at seeing her here. Only that terse greeting, as if— Her fingers curled into fists. As if he'd half expected her.

A tidal wave of emotions crashed through Chloe. Like a huge, onrushing breaker, it swept everything along with it, including the shadows that had haunted her for so many weeks. She almost staggered under alternating surges of hurt, savage jealousy, fierce possessiveness.

The hurt and the jealousy washed away after the first few waves. Only the possessiveness remained, as raw and elemental as the sexes. One thought burned in her brain. One absolute certainty blazed in her chest. Mase was hers. He loved her. She loved him. Whatever had occurred between him and this woman had nothing to do with his feelings for Chloe. Nothing to do with what just happened up at the lake.

Nothing!

Or so she tried to convince herself when Pam stopped beside Mase, her face every bit as grim as his.

"Dexter Greene is in the area."

"The hell he is!"

"He was in Rapid City on Wednesday."

"Wednesday! Two days ago! And you're just telling me about it?"

"The damned bureaucrats at the Bureau didn't pass the word until this morning." Her mouth twisted into a snarl. "I can personally guarantee they'll be more efficient the next time."

"There won't be a next time," Mase promised in a tone that raised the hairs on the back of Chloe's neck.

Pam threw a quick glance over her shoulder, then lowered her voice. Still stiff, still swamped by the savage possessiveness that rooted her to the spot, Chloe caught a hurried reference to the Chief, whoever that was, and a team standing by for Mase's orders.

"We've got to get this operation in gear," the brunette finished in a hurried undertone, slanting another quick look at Chloe. "Jackson's inside. He can stay with Miss Fortune until you're briefed, and we'll work out how we're going to pick up Greene's trail. We need you, Mase. Now."

The face he turned to Chloe stunned her. This wasn't the man who'd spent two days with her counting cans of cat food. Or even the man who'd just taken her to a soaring, searing passion. This was a stranger, iron hard and razor-edged. Even his voice was different, as sharp as ground glass.

"Give me a minute, Pam."

"Mase..."

"Give me a minute."

She chopped the air with one hand, as if wanting to argue the matter, then conceded with stiff reluctance. "I'll let Jackson know we're leaving Miss Fortune with him."

Chloe's chin snapped up. She didn't like being "left," any more than she liked being dismissed by this sleek, too-confident female. Nor did she make the least effort to hide her anger. Her eyes locked on the other woman's as she made for the steps.

Pam blinked, her confident stride faltering for a fraction of a second. Then she swept into the store, leaving Chloe alone with the man whose arms had held her so tenderly not an hour ago. He didn't display the least sign of tenderness now. He didn't display anything except a tight-jawed urgency. With an eerie sense of déjà vu, she stood as stiff as one of the store's porch supports while Mase closed the short distance between them.

"Chloe, listen to me. You've got to trust me. I can't explain what's going on here."

She choked. That had a familiar ring to it. She was still struggling with a fresh surge of memories when his fingers closed around her upper arms. Frustration and a racing urgency showed plainly in his face.

"I can't explain because I don't *know* what's going on here. All I can tell you is that we suspect a man named Dexter Greene may be tracking me."

"Tracking you?"

"Stalking," he corrected grimly. "He's dangerous, Chloe. Very dangerous."

"But how…? Why…?"

"I need details, need to understand the situation. I'll come back as soon as I'm briefed and tell you everything I can, I promise."

"Everything you can? That's not good enough."

"It has to be."

"No." Her hands came up to ball against his chest. "I'm not settling for a few, carefully selected crumbs. I want it all, Mase. I want every memory, every bit of our past. Every bit of *your* past. If we're going to share that future we talked about, there can't be any more shadows or secrets between us."

"We're going to share more than a future." His fingers dug into her flesh. "I love you, Chloe. Only you. I want to marry you. I want to make babies with you. I want to grow old and potbellied and gray with you. Trust me, sweetheart. Please. For a little while longer."

Chloe didn't intend to cave. She wanted explanations. Needed explanations. But the urgency in Mase's voice cut deep into her stubborn determination. The expression in his eyes sliced right through it. Startled, Chloe thought she caught a fleeting glimpse of worry behind the love in their gray depths.

Or was it fear? For her? For himself? Shaken, she

conceded. "All right. I'll wait a little while longer, but…"

Before she could add any conditions or caveats, he hauled her up against him. His mouth came down on hers, hard and fast and so consuming that the world seemed to spin right off its axis. For a moment the only real objects in the universe were her and Mase and the endless blue sky above them. She clung to him, needing an anchor, needing his solid strength, needing the bedrock of his love. Far too soon for her peace of mind, he used his grip on her arms to break the contact.

"Go inside, Chloe. Stay there. Pam will introduce you to a man named Dave Jackson. He'll stay with you until I get back."

She got as far as the porch steps. She turned, wanting to urge him to be careful. The words died on her lips. Gulping, she watched Mase remove a small leather holster from the Blazer's dash compartment.

With a swift economy of movement that told her he'd done it many times before, he drew a lethal looking weapon from the holster, snapped out its magazine, checked the load and shoved the clip back in place. Grim-faced, he holstered the weapon and reached into the dash again. He was checking the spare magazine when he glanced up and saw her frozen in place.

"Go inside, Chloe. Stay there."

*   *   *

She went inside.

Charlie Thomas was waiting for her, a look of confusion on his heavyset face. So was Pam Hawkins and another man Chloe had never seen before. Impatience in every line of her body, Pam introduced a scarecrow-thin individual with a shy smile and a shock of frizzy blond hair.

"This is Dave Jackson. Don't be fooled by his appearance. He's one of our best."

"One of *whose* best?"

The acidly polite question fell on deaf ears. "Mase will tell you what he can, when he can." Turning to the man at her side, Pam issued a brusque instruction. "You've got your radio. Call me or Mase if you need us."

"Will do." Jackson grinned, his thin face folding accordionlike into well worn grooves. "This is just like old times, isn't it? The team all together again. You and Mase playing the game hard and fast and rough, the way you always did."

The brunette sent Chloe a swift, slanting glance. "Close enough," she murmured. "Close enough."

"No, it's not."

Chloe's low growl surprised her almost as much as it did the other three. As soon as the words were out, though, she knew they were right.

Like a rush of images on a rewinding VCR, memories spilled through her. She saw herself running from Mase's office. Running out of the high-rise building. Running for her Mercedes, a loaded weekend bag in her hand and an ache in her heart.

Well, she wasn't running anymore. And she damned well wasn't letting this woman think she could play any kind of games with Mase. She moved forward until they stood toe-to-toe.

"Nothing's the same," Chloe informed the woman in a voice as impenetrable as steel. "Whatever happened between you and Mase in the past, nothing will ever be the same again."

Catlike brown eyes narrowed. "You think so?"

"I know so."

For long moments Pam stared at her. Chloe had just decided the other woman wasn't going to respond when Pam nodded. It was a tiny movement, barely perceptible. Her chin dipped only a few degrees. Yet that small movement signaled defeat and a vulnerability that blew away some of the rancor that hovered like a living thing between the two women.

Chloe saw in that instant that Pam loved him. In her own way, she loved him. The realization gave her the courage to reach out and lay her hand on the other woman's arm.

"Be careful."

Pam glanced down. When she looked up again, her smile almost reached her eyes.

"I will."

She left in a whirl of expensive perfume and another spate of instructions to Jackson. Chloe fought the urge to follow her and say a last goodbye to Mase. He didn't need further distractions. He'd come back to her when he could. He'd promised. In the meantime, she desperately craved some time and some quiet to deal with the memories imploding in on her. First, though, she had to check on Hannah.

"I'm sorry we were gone so long, Charlie. Is Hannah all right?"

The retired postal worker nodded. "She's fine. A little disgruntled over the fact that she can't get up to check out all these strangers who've come to town, but otherwise fine."

"Thanks again for staying with her."

Rubbing his jowls, the postal worker measured Dave Jackson from his frizzy hair to his black-toed boots. "I can stay longer, if you need me."

"It's not necessary."

When the door closed behind him, the gangly Jackson gave Chloe another shy smile. "You go do what you need to do, Miss Fortune. I'll mind the store. Pam and I checked it out while we were waiting for you. The living quarters, too. I can get to you in a heartbeat if I need to."

With that somewhat dubious assurance ringing in her ears, Chloe threaded through the crowded storeroom to the private quarters beyond. As expected, she found Hannah with her arms folded across her chest and a ferocious scowl on her sun-weathered face.

"What's goin' on here, girl?"

"I wish I knew."

Chloe dropped into one of the armchairs, almost as exhausted by the emotions of the past few minutes as by the hours at the lake.

"That Hawkins woman flashed an ID under my nose," Hannah grumbled. "Said she and Mase were trackin' some kind of dangerous nut. I don't need any piece of plastic to see that she's packin' trouble along with her sleek hair and too slick ways."

"More kinds of trouble than you think."

Hannah's sharp ears picked up the strain in her voice.

"So she's the one," she muttered obscurely. Her gaze focused on Chloe. "Do you know this woman?"

"Me? No. But Mase..."

She chewed on her lower lip. Despite her brave words to Pam a few minutes ago, doubts began to buzz around her like annoying little gnats. The brunette obviously considered Mase more than a partner. Just as obviously she wanted to rekindle whatever relationship they once shared. Did Mase want that, too?

Hannah's snort blew her doubts right out of the air.

"Any damn fool with eyes in his head could see

that Mason Chandler loves you, child. And from the grass and bits of leaves stuck in your hair, I'd say he spent his time up at the lake showin' you just how much.''

An embarrassed grin pulled at Chloe's lips. ''I think I showed him a thing or two or three, too.''

''Hmmmm.''

Hannah digested that, then pinned Chloe with a sharp look. ''Did he tell you that you found this Hawkins woman in his arms? That she's the reason you ran away from him?''

Her brief spurt of amusement dimmed. ''He didn't have to tell me. I remembered.''

''You remembered?'' Hannah shot upright on her sofa. ''Everything?''

''Almost everything. It's coming back to me in spurts.''

''I knew you'd do it, girl!'' Overjoyed, the older woman held out her hand. ''I never had any doubt!''

Chloe slipped off her chair and knelt beside the sofa. Folding her fingers around her employer's, she raised her hand to her cheek.

''Maybe you didn't have any doubts, but I did. At times, the shadows were so thick and dark I thought I'd never find my way out of them. I...I couldn't have made it through these weeks without you, Hannah.''

The display of gratitude drew another snort from the older woman, this one of embarrassed pleasure.

She tut-tutted and pooh-poohed and hmmmmed, but didn't draw her hand away. Something suspiciously close to tears sheened her blue eyes when she finally told her employee not to act so foolish.

"You're tougher than you think you are, Chloe Fortune. You would've found your way back to your man sooner or later. Now get up off that floor and go comb your hair."

With a smile and wave to Hannah, she retraced her steps to the storeroom. When she caught sight of the haphazardly stacked boxes and jumble of old goods waiting to be shelved, her steps slowed. A frown etched across her brow. Slowly, she trailed a hand along an unopened carton of fruit juice.

Regaining her memory meant losing the sanctuary she'd found in Crockett. She would return to Minneapolis with Mase, go back to her family and the busy life she'd led before. And leave the woman who'd become her friend as well as her employer.

Who would carry these heavy cartons into the store for Hannah until her ankle bones knit? Who'd deal with that stack of unpaid bills she pretended didn't exist? Who'd handle the suppliers and rotate the produce and close up at night?

Charlie Thomas? Doc Johnson? Mayor Dobbins? Everyone in town loved Hannah. They should, considering that she supplied their needs at prices that barely covered her costs. They could help. They'd have to help. Chloe was working out a schedule of volunteers in her mind when the sound of footsteps coming toward the storeroom thudded through the stillness. Her heart jumped.

Mase! Maybe it was Mase! She hadn't heard the bell jangle. She flew across the storeroom and through the door to the store…only to almost smack into the man rounding the end of the counter.

Hard hands reached out to steady her. She caught a waft of cigarette-tainted breath and knew even before she looked up that the man who held her wasn't Mase. She pulled out of his hold, recognizing him immediately. The lone diner from the café. Last night's late customer. His smoke-yellowed eyes identified him as surely as his scraggly hair. Shaking free of his hold, she stepped back.

"I'm sorry," she gasped. "I didn't mean to plow into you."

He flicked a quick glance over her shoulder into the storeroom before answering in a slow drawl. "No harm done, ma'am."

His brown eyes came back to her, assessing, almost calculating in their intentness. The uneasiness that had pinged at Chloe last night in this man's presence came swooping back. This time, it carried the added kick of Mase's startling revelations.

Someone was stalking him.

Someone dangerous.

She darted a look past the man's red hunting vest, searching the store for Dave Jackson. All she saw

were dust motes dancing on the late-afternoon sun-
beams and the empty area around the stove. Her
uneasiness spiked into sudden, sweaty fear. Some
latent survival instinct made her strive to keep her
fear hidden.

"Did you...?"

Despite her best efforts, her voice wobbled. She
swallowed and moved as casually as she could toward the counter. She wanted to put that solid ex-
panse of wood between them.

"Did you come in for more cigarette fixings?"

"No, ma'am. I came for you."

The words held such total lack of inflection that
it took a few seconds for their message to sink in.
When it did, Chloe spun around to confront him.
Incredulous, she saw that he'd followed hard on her
heels. Instead of separating them, the counter now
trapped her in the enclosed space. He didn't smile,
didn't display any outward emotion at all. But Chloe
saw his intent in his eyes.

She opened her mouth to scream.

Before she could get out much more than a strangled squawk, his fist smashed into her jaw. Her
knees gave out, and she felt herself toppling backward. A second later, the world pitched into darkness.

Ten

"Tell me how you know Dexter Greene was in Rapid City two days ago."

Tense and wired tight, Mase fired the curt order at Pam. She answered with the cool professionalism that had saved both her skin and his more than once.

"The FBI intercepted a call from Greene's daughter-in-law to a friend. Sharon Greene let drop that her father-in-law had contacted her Wednesday morning. Once the Bureau passed on that interesting tidbit, it took only a few hours for us to check the record of her incoming calls. One of those calls traced to a phone booth in Rapid City."

Mase paced his rented room, where Pam and her

small team had gathered to brief him. He felt as caged and constrained as the trophies Mayor Dobbins had mounted on the wall.

Small to begin with, the room now overflowed with Pam and two additional team members, plus their assorted pursuit and tracking equipment. The specially designed and fitted boxes were stacked against the walls. Each case contained the latest in high-tech gadgetry, including compact satellite dishes and transceivers, night vision equipment, weapons fitted with infrared scopes and laser beam sights, and lightweight Kevlar protective gear. The team had come prepared to take down a potential killer.

Mase studied the cases, his heart pumping pure adrenaline as it always did during a mission. This time, though, it also pumped a worry that ate like battery acid at his gut. Despite the doctor's orders not to rush Chloe or force her to face her past before she was ready, Mase knew they'd both just run out of time. He had to get her out of Crockett, out of the line of fire.

Then he'd go after Dexter Greene.

"Call in a helo," he instructed Pam tersely. "As soon as we finish here, I'll drive Chloe to the landing site. I want to get her away from here before any shooting starts."

"I've already set up an extraction," his partner

replied with a small smile. "The bird will be waiting when you and Chloe get there."

"Good. What else have you got?"

A thirty-year-old with a roly-poly chubbiness that made her look more like a slightly overweight coed than the highly skilled agent she was flipped open her laptop computer.

"We know Greene's using one or more aliases. He's also disguised himself. The clerk at the rental car agency in Minneapolis couldn't remember him very well—evidently he hit the counter at a peak period—but she gave me a few vague descriptive details to run through the composite database. According to the rental car agent, he's dyed his hair gray." The pudgy operative hit the keys. Greene's face as Mase had first seen it materialized on the screen. With a click of a key, Greene's hair turned white. "He let it grow longer and grew a beard."

"Hold it!"

Mase barked the order so sharply the operative jumped half out of her chair. Her fingers skittered on the keys, jumbling the picture.

"Back up an image," he snapped. "One more. There! Hold it there!"

He leaned over her shoulder, his blood congealing in his veins. He'd seen that face. Those yellowish-tinted eyes. Recently. As recently as...

Last night!

This man was one of the diners who'd turned out

for Mayor Dobbins's rib-eye special. A loner. Hunched over a table in the far corner. Mase was sure of it!

The solitary diner was thinner than the individual in this computer-enhanced photo. Far thinner. His cheeks had caved in, giving him the appearance of a much older man, and his hair scraggled down his neck. Those yellowish-tinted eyes had lifted for just a second when he and Chloe passed, but...

Chloe! Greene had seen him with Chloe!

Mase bolted for the door.

"He's here, in Crockett," he snarled at the startled crew. "He saw me last night with Chloe. I've got to get her out of here."

"I'll back you up." Pam scrambled to her feet, spitting orders to the other two as she charged out the door hard on Mase's heels. "Get into position. Give us a cross-quadrant cover of the general store and main street. Move, dammit, move!"

The instant Pam threw herself into the passenger seat, Mase shoved the Blazer into gear and took off, tires squealing. Alternately cursing and praying, he laid a strip of rubber all the way up the street. The Blazer almost climbed up the front steps of the store before it screeched to a stop.

Mase raced up the remaining steps. The door flew open. The bell crashed and jangled. A white-haired, white-faced Hannah spun awkwardly on her crutches and leveled her double-barreled shotgun square at his midsection.

"Damn, boy!" she growled. "You just about got yourself air-conditioned."

"Where's Chloe?"

"And Dave Jackson?" Pam snapped, pushing in behind him.

"I don't know." Hannah lowered the shotgun, her weathered face folding into sharp creases. "I heard a funny noise. A squeak or a squawk or something. I called out, but no one answered, so I hauled my carcass out of bed to investigate."

"What did you find?"

"Nothing so far, but I can't maneuver these damned crutches enough to get through the aisles." Her blue eyes telegraphed a worry she didn't try to hide. "I thought…I hoped maybe Chloe was with you."

"She's not. Check the store, Pam. I'll take the back room and the upstairs."

Mase was halfway to the storeroom when Pam's shout stopped him in his tracks.

"Mase! Here!"

Spinning, he sprinted to a dusty corner at the back of the store. Dave Jackson lay in a crumpled heap, his body hidden behind fifty-pound bags of rock salt. Enough blood had flowed from the gaping wound at the back of his skull to stain the floorboards beneath him a dark crimson.

"He's alive," Pam reported, her fingers on the pulse point under his jaw.

Mase dropped to one knee to examine the wound. Fear for Chloe clawed at his chest, but the rules he'd set for himself in dozens of desperate missions couldn't be ignored. Rule one, never leave a buddy in the field. Rule two, see that the injured got priority attention. Rule three, haul ass when the air filled with too many flying bullets to dodge.

Rule three didn't apply in this case, Mase thought grimly. He wasn't hauling anything anywhere until he found Chloe.

To his intense relief, Dave stirred and gave a small groan. The wound at the back of his skull showed broken skin and bruising, but no bits of bone or brain matter. He'd make it.

"Call in a medical team," Mase instructed, surging to his feet. "Stay with him until someone gets here."

He left Pam fumbling for her radio and raced for the storeroom. He found what he was looking for mere seconds later. An unlocked back door. A set of man's boot prints in the dirt outside the door. But no blood. Thank God, no blood.

The prints had sunk deep in the dirt, as though their owner carried a heavy burden. They trailed across the open area behind the store, then disappeared into the pines. His heart pounding, Mase stared at the dense screen of pines. A chilling image formed of an unconscious Chloe slung across Dexter Greene's shoulder. Of Chloe helpless, maybe traumatized from a blow to her head.

His chin jerked up as a new fear jolted through him. What had the neurologist said? That another shock or trauma could cause amnesia victims to retreat even further? That her memory loss could become permanent?

Ruthlessly Mase shoved the bleak possibility aside. He couldn't worry about that now. Right now he had to deal with the more distinct possibility that Dexter Greene had carried Chloe into the Black Hills....

Did he intend to use her as bait to draw Mase into a net? Or to make him suffer the same agony of loss he had suffered?

The cold sweat prickling Mase's skin turned to ice. Savagely, he shook off his suffocating fear for Chloe. He needed to focus, do what he'd been trained to do. A few swift strides took him back inside the store.

"I found his footprints. I'm going after him."

Pam glanced up from where she knelt beside Dave, a swift frown forming. One look at Mase killed whatever protest she'd been about to make. Instead, she simply nodded.

"I'll follow with the others. We'll be right behind you."

"Here," Hannah said gruffly, passing him the shotgun. "Take this with you."

She juggled her crutch and reached into her pocket. A moment later, a box of shells sailed through the air. Mase caught them one-handed.

"If that bastard's hurt Chloe," she said fiercely, "you tote his hide back here for Harold Dobbins to cure."

"If he's hurt Chloe, there won't be enough left of his hide to cure."

Chloe came awake to the oddest sensations. The left side of her jaw felt like a swinging door had smacked into it. Her shoulder joints were on fire. Her wrists burned where they were bound together behind her back. She ached all the way across her middle, as though she'd pulled a belt too tight or bent over an iron bar. Even worse, her skin prickled all over with goose bumps.

It took only a moment to locate the source of the goose bumps. They sprang from the long shadows cast by the pines, which hid the slowly sinking sun and sucked the warmth from the granite cliffs that surrounded her.

It took only a moment longer to locate the source of Chloe's other discomforts. He was crouched on one knee a few yards away, shielded behind a granite outcropping. His ball cap rode low on his forehead. His eyes were locked on a faint path that wound through the trees below the cliffs. A high-powered hunting rifle rested on the flat surface of a boulder.

Suddenly and completely wide-awake, Chloe felt the icy drench of terror. Desperately she fought to free herself of its grip.

She wouldn't panic! she swore on a silent sob. She wouldn't! She'd breathe deeply. Choke down her swamping fear. Pray that Mase came soon. Push herself away from her captor, inch by—

"Aaah!"

Her first, tentative movement brought a cry ripping from her throat. White-hot needles shot from her shoulder sockets, raced down her arms, centered on her bound wrists. She fell back, gasping, as her captor swiveled a few degrees on his heel.

"Awake, are you?"

He didn't leave his post or abandon his weapon. The path through the trees remained in his line of vision. With senses heightened by sheer terror, Chloe absorbed the details she hadn't picked up on the night before.

The drawling accent, so different from that of the South Dakotans. The sunken cheeks. The utter implacability in his eyes.

"Sorry I had to hurt you, ma'am. I don't hold with hurting women as a rule, but I knew that taking you was the surest way to get your man in my gun sights."

In his sights. Oh, God! He was waiting for Mase. He planned to shoot him!

Chloe's silent prayer that Mase would come charging to her rescue suddenly became a fervent, fervid plea for him to stay away, to keep safe. Ignoring the agony in her tightly bound arms, she hitched onto her hip, then up on one elbow. Panting and on fire from her neck to her wrists, she finally rolled upright. A moment later she sagged against the granite wall behind her.

"Why..." She fought to get the words through a throat dry with fear. "Why are you after him? What did he do to you?"

"He killed my son."

The stark reply staggered Chloe. For a stunned moment she could only gape at him.

"No!" she burst out. "No, you're wrong! Mase wouldn't kill anyone! He couldn't!"

The brown irises swimming in the yellowish whites grew flatter, colder. "He could. He did."

"You're after the wrong man!" She got a leg under her, steadying herself. "I don't know how your son died or why you think Mase killed him, but I know he wouldn't—"

"My boy died in a cell, gutted like a pig. Your man tracked him down and put him there. He and that bitch he works with. He's worse than the bounty hunters who used to roam these hills, even if he does work for the U.S. government."

"Mase?" Chloe said faintly. "Are you talking about Mason Chandler?"

Her captor spit a brownish stream at the ground. "He didn't call himself Mason Chandler when he snaked his way into our compound. He didn't look all smooth and polished like he does now, either. They drugged my boy and carried him off to die in that cell. It took me two years to learn his real name. Two years to find him."

Chloe stared at him, incredulous. Surely he had the wrong man! Surely he couldn't be talking about Mase! Solid, steady Mase! Yet he seemed so absolutely convinced. And… She swallowed. And Mase traveled so much.

Memories sliced through her disbelief and mind-numbing fear. Of her fiancé just back from one of his extended business trips, his cheeks haggard and the skin under his eyes bluish with a fatigue that couldn't have come from boardroom meetings. Of the time she called him on what she considered a matter of some urgency, only to be put on hold while her call was transferred with a series of discreet clicks to some distant location.

Suddenly Chloe conjured up another image, this one of a blue sky and a tiny lake and a small, puckered scar in Mase's naked shoulder. He'd laughed it off. She'd gotten so lost in the magic of his hands and mouth on her body that she'd let him. Only now did it occur to her that the hole in his shoulder had come from a bullet.

For a crazy moment the earth seemed to tremor under her. The universe she'd just begun piecing together again shifted, then fell apart once more. The memories that had come rushing back to her such a short time ago had centered around the Mase Chandler she thought she knew. Now she realized in stunned disbelief, she didn't know him at all. She'd never really known him.

Her shock showed plainly to her captor. His lips pulled back in a small, satisfied smile.

"You had no idea what Chandler did when he left his fancy office, did you, missy? You ought to thank me. I'm saving you from marrying a killer."

Chloe stared at him, aghast. Her mouth opened, closed, opened again. "No! I don't— I can't— Oh, God, I just can't believe that Mase...my Mase..."

Ever afterward she would give regular and fervent thanks for her stuttering incoherence. It seemed to amuse her captor. It certainly deepened the intensity of his satisfaction. Even more important, it diverted his attention for a second or two...just long enough for Chloe to catch the sudden movement of the shadow thrown against the cliff face behind him.

Her babbling became more desperate, more strident.

"You've followed the wrong man. Mase isn't a killer. He wouldn't hurt anyone."

She used the leg bent under her to push herself up on one knee. The shadow painted on the cliff behind her captor shifted again.

"I know Mase," she cried. "I love him. He's not a killer."

Then, in a few split seconds, the world around her erupted into violence.

A boot scraped on rock.

Her captor swore, snatched up his rifle, swung around.

A shot exploded at the exact instant Chloe threw herself across the rocks.

She crashed into her kidnapper, taking him down with her just as Mase dropped from the cliff above. Blinded by a cloud of stinging cordite, deafened by the crack of the rifle, she used her forehead and her shoulder and her knee to inflict what damage she could on her captor before she was thrust violently against the rocks.

By the time a wash of tears had cleared the burning cordite, her kidnapper lay sprawled across the rocks. Mase crouched over him, his chest heaving. For a second, just a second, Chloe saw murder in his eyes.

Her heart froze.

Was it true? Was he a killer?

Before she could speak, before she could even draw a breath, he whipped off his belt and flipped the man onto his face with brutal disregard for his unconscious state. A few quick twists of the belt lashed her attacker's wrists together.

Then Mase, her Mase, turned and gathered her in his arms.

Eleven

Never, ever, would Chloe have believed that the terror and violence she'd just experienced could produce bright, shining moments she would savor forever.

The first moment came when Mase took her in his arms. Voice shaking, hands trembling, he cradled her against his chest.

"Chloe, baby, are you hurt? Did he hurt you?"

She blinked to clear the last of her tears, only to blink again at the fierce, unrelenting love on his face.

"I'm not hurt."

Much. She bit back a wince as he rocked her

against his chest. White-hot needles shot up and down her bound arms.

"Mase. Please, my wrists."

Somehow she wasn't surprised when he produced a deadly looking knife from nowhere and sawed through the duct tape binding her arms. Gently he drew her limp arms forward.

Not so gently, he began to massage them.

"Ow!"

Chloe abandoned any and all attempts at heroic fortitude as pain needled her numb limbs.

"I know it feels as if you've got glass in your veins," he said, his voice rough and tender at the same time. "But this will get the blood circulating faster."

She scrunched her eyes shut, enduring the agony as blood pumped back into her flesh. Mase finished one arm and went to work on the other. Slowly, achingly, feeling crept back into her limbs.

Pam Hawkins's arrival on the scene speeded the process considerably. The brunette burst out of the trees, weapon drawn and held two-fisted before her. Two complete strangers charged behind her, similarly armed. All three skidded to a stop when they spotted Mase and Chloe.

"We heard a shot," Pam panted. Her glance swept to the figure sprawled unconscious on the rocks. "That's Greene all right. Dammit, Mase, you should have waited for backup to bring him down."

"I didn't bring him down. Chloe did."

The brunette's reaction provided the second, shining moment, one Chloe would savor for years. Stunned out of her seemingly unshakable cool, Pam gaped at the kidnappee.

Chloe tried. She really tried not to smirk. She wasn't totally successful, but she did manage to bite back the snide little observation that Hawkins wasn't the only one who could play hard and fast and rough when necessary.

The third moment came a few hours later, after a small army of law enforcement officials had descended on Crockett by land vehicle and helicopter. Using Mayor Dobbins's café as a sort of impromptu command post, they took custody of a swearing, handcuffed Dexter Greene. Chloe gave her statement, then stood on the sidelines as Mase briefed them on the background leading up to the afternoon's events.

This was another Mase, another one she hadn't seen before. He wore a bruise high on his left cheek from direct contact with Greene's rifle butt. His dark hair sported an assortment of pine needles and a layer of dust. The jagged rocks had ripped out one knee of his jeans, and his blue shirt had taken as much of a beating as he had during the desperate struggle. Yet he carried himself with an air of crisp authority that the others instinctively deferred to…and he certainly knew far more about the apprehension and disposition of criminals than your everyday, average business executive.

The state and federal officers took Dexter Greene with them when they left. Pam Hawkins and her team departed a short time later in a whir of chopper blades and flashing strobe lights that cut through the rapidly descending mountain darkness like knives.

The small crowd of residents who'd gathered to find out what all the fuss was about retreated inside the café. Even Hannah, whom Mase had driven down from the store, joined the group. Exclamations circulated as fast and as freely as the ice-cold beers, with half the population asserting that Greene had looked suspicious from the first moment they'd laid eyes on him, while the other half shook their heads and wondered what the world was coming to. Chloe made sure Hannah was settled comfortably with her friends before she detached Mase from the loquacious group.

"I need to talk to you. Privately. Can we go upstairs?"

"We can," he replied, his gray eyes glinting behind their screen of black lashes. "I'll give you the same warning I gave you last time, though. If I take you upstairs, I'm not promising I'll keep my hands off you."

The less-than-subtle warning had made Chloe shy

off a few nights ago. This time she matched him gleam for gleam.

"Did I ask for any promises?"

Mase sucked in a sharp breath, then hustled her out of the café and up the stairs so swiftly that the residents of Crockett stared at them in astonishment. All except Hannah. Chloe caught the tail end of the grin that creased her employer's weathered face before she turned to the mayor/bartender and demanded another beer.

Once they reached his room, Chloe turned to Mase. "I think you should know my memory's come back," she said.

"Chloe!"

Delight and relief lit his eyes. He was halfway across the room before he absorbed her militant stance and the cool note in her voice. He stopped a few feet away, regret and a wary sort of caution in his face.

"I wanted to explain about Pam, Chloe. I had an explanation all ready, but you took off before I could lay it on you." His lips twisted. "I guess it's just as well. The story I'd patched together was a careful collection of lies and half-truths."

"I don't want lies and half-truths between us. No fake engagements. No shadows from our past. No secret lives. Ever again."

"Pam isn't between us. She never was."

Chloe dismissed the doubts and insecurities that

had plagued her all those weeks ago with an impatient wave of one hand.

"I know that now. I guess I knew it then. It's taken me a while to figure it out, but I realize now I didn't run away because I found Pam draped all over you, Mase. I ran away because I'd fallen in love with you. No, that's not true. I'd fallen in love with someone I didn't even know! A secret agent, for heaven's sake!"

"I'm not making any excuses. I did what I did for so many years because—" he lifted a shoulder in a small shrug "—it needed to be done. I couldn't tell you about it. I couldn't tell anyone. That was part of our code."

"No! You don't understand! I don't blame you. I blame myself. All this time, all these months we've been engaged, I was so selfish, so self-absorbed, so damned blind! I never guessed, never even had a clue what you were up to during those extended business trips."

Mase couldn't help himself. She looked so thoroughly disgusted that he had to reach for her. She came into his arms still stiff, still militant.

"It wouldn't say a whole lot for my image of myself as the nineties' answer to James Bond if you'd picked up what I did during those trips."

"This isn't a joke! How could I love you when I never saw the real you? How could you love *me?*"

"Chloe, darling, you weren't supposed to see the real me."

"That's no excuse. I feel so…so stupid!"

"If it helps any, I feel pretty stupid, too."

"You? Why?"

"I should have spotted Greene." His voice roughened. "I should never have let him get to you. The last thing I wanted was to expose you to this kind of danger. I'm sorry, so sorry."

"You're forgiven. This time." A shiver rippled through her as she remembered the malevolent look in Greene's eyes just before he was led away. "I'm not sure I'll be so forgiving next time, though."

"There won't be a next time. I quit the agency, Chloe. Months ago. I decided you were far more important to me than what I did before."

"You did?" She hiked a brow. "Was that why Pam came to Minneapolis? To entice you back into playing—how did she put it?—hard and fast and rough with her?"

Mase felt a flush creep up his cheeks. Her memory had returned, all right.

"That was one of the reasons," he answered with brutal honesty. He wouldn't lie to her. Not anymore. "The other was to brief me on Greene."

She thought about that for a moment or two. Mase found himself holding his breath. Would she believe him? Could she trust him after all these months of subterfuge?

He'd started to sweat by the time she uncrossed her arms and slid one hand up to pluck a long, dry pine needle from his hair. Twirling the brittle spike between her fingers, she gazed at it thoughtfully.

"I take it your resignation means you won't be taking any more extended trips?"

"Not without you."

She tossed the pine sprig aside. Her violet eyes filled with a love that knocked Mase's heart all around his rib cage. "Good! Because the next trip we take is going to be our honeymoon."

Grinning, he bent down to brush her lips with his. "Let's go somewhere with lots of sun and blue sky and sparkling lakes."

"Funny," she murmured against his mouth. "That sounds a lot like Crockett."

"So it does." In one quick sweep, he had her up in his arms. "If you're willing to risk making love under that rack of antlers, I'm all for starting our honeymoon right here, right now."

Smiling, she framed his cheeks with her palms. "Right here, right now sounds pretty good to me."

When he planted a knee on the narrow bed and lowered her to the chenille spread, the springs creaked. They groaned in earnest when Mase shed his clothes and joined her a few moments later.

Slowly, deliberately, he peeled off her top. Slowly, torturously, he took down her jeans and panties. His tongue found her navel, her breasts, her throat. Finally, he worked his way to her mouth. Her toes curling in delight, Chloe added a few groans of her own to those of the bedsprings.

Her hands were as busy as his, her mouth as warm and willing. She was ready long before Mase. More than ready. Wet and eager and on fire with a need that went far beyond physical, she opened herself to him.

He settled his weight between her thighs, and the rest of the world faded from her vision. The intimidating stag mounted above the bed blurred. The scrubbed pine walls disappeared. The world narrowed, centered, joined, until there was only Mase.

She held nothing back. Nor did he. Their loving was so deep, so all consuming, that Chloe knew she'd never again feel lost or confused or alone.

By the time they lay limp and exhausted, she wasn't sure she'd ever feel *anything* again. Her body was numb from pleasure, her mind languorous. Her arms and legs tangled with Mase's, as much to keep from tumbling off the narrow bed as to maintain contact with the man who filled her heart as well as her soul.

With some effort, she pried open her eyes. Above her, the stag gazed down at their sweat-slicked bodies with what looked very much like amusement. Chloe grinned back at him. This could, she decided in lazy, sensual satisfaction, stretch into a *very* long honeymoon.

At which point it occurred to her that they ought to think about a wedding. Which, naturally, led to a tumble of thoughts about the extravagant ceremony she'd been roped into planning and the invitations Mollie was waiting to send out and her father's stew over what to buy them for a wedding present.

Her father. Chloe smiled, her heart overflowing with memories. Her elbow poked the sweaty chest behind her.

"Mase."

"Mmmm."

"I need to call my father."

He mumbled something into her hair about not having either the energy or the fortitude to face Emmet at this moment, even by phone. Nevertheless, he untangled his legs, rolled off the bed and pulled on his jeans. Retrieving his shirt and a small portable phone, he handed both to Chloe.

"This is one call I'm not looking forward to," he admitted wryly. "Your father isn't going to appreciate the fact that I almost got you killed."

"Then we won't tell him."

She poked her arms through the shirtsleeves. A few moments later, she cradled the cell phone to her ear, crying, laughing, feeling completely whole at last as her father poured out a torrent of love, long-suppressed worry and instructions.

"I'm sending a plane out for you," Emmet boomed. "It'll be airborne two minutes after we hang up. Come home, Chloe. Come home and stay home. Marry Mase and make lots of babies and don't ever put me through what I've gone through these past weeks again."

"I plan to marry Mase, Daddy." She flashed a smile at the bridegroom under discussion. "I also plan to make lots of babies."

"Good! I'll tell Mollie to send out the wedding invitations."

"Tell her to take care of the rest of the arrangements, too."

"What?"

"She'll have to take care of all the details. I won't be home for a while yet."

Emmet's violent protest exploded in her ear. Wincing, Chloe held the phone a few inches away while several secondary detonations took place. Finally the noise level at the other end of the line had died enough for her to be heard.

"I can't leave Crockett. Not yet."

"Why not?"

"I have to make sure Hannah's taken care of."

"Hannah! Who the hell's Hannah?"

"Hannah Crockett. She's the proprietor of the general store where I've been working. I owe her for..."

"We'll pay whatever you owe ten times over! In cash. I want you home."

"No, Daddy," she said gently. "Cash won't come close to compensating for the comfort and security and friendship Hannah gave me. I have to see that she gets to Rapid City to get the pins in her ankle removed and arrange for someone to cover the store and—"

She stopped, startled by the idea that suddenly sprang into her mind. It spun through her head, picking up speed and brilliance like a dazzling, pinwheeling Fourth of July firecracker. Held in thrall by the idea, Chloe glanced at Mase. She should talk this through with him, explore the possibilities, look at the potential.

No, she didn't have to talk it over. Not with Mase. He'd supported her desire to break into the business world when her own father hadn't taken her seriously. He would support her in this, too. The idea was still taking shape when Emmet burst impatiently into her thoughts.

"And what, Chloe? What do you have to do that's so damned important it takes precedence over planning your wedding?"

With a wide smile for the half-naked man across the room, she dropped her bomb.

"I have to talk to Hannah about buying a partnership in her store."

Mase's brows shot up. As quickly as Chloe herself had, he explored the possibilities. By the time Emmet had finished sputtering and issuing dire warnings about two-bit operations and losing propositions, she saw only approval and encouragement in Mase's smile.

If she hadn't already loved Mase, she would have fallen for him at that moment, and fallen hard. His expression said more clearly than words that they were a team from here on out. He was with her in whatever enterprise she wanted to undertake. Her heart brimming with happiness, Chloe cut off her father's demand to know if she'd lost her mind.

"The Crockett General Store doesn't have to remain a two-bit operation, Dad. With a little strategic planning and some targeted advertising, we could capture more of the tourist trade. We could also add some gourmet items," she continued, thinking hard and fast. "Maybe even franchise."

"Franchise!"

Emmet went ballistic once more. Mase, bless his heart, took pity on her. Strolling across the room, he held out his hand. Chloe passed him the phone in relief. With cheerful ruthlessness, he cut through her father's impassioned speech about profit and loss statements.

"Your daughter's a Fortune, Emmet. For a little while longer, anyway. She knows what she's doing."

That silenced her father for a few precious seconds. It also earned Mase a very long, very passionate kiss. One kiss led to another and another. Abruptly Mase snapped the cell phone to his ear.

"We'll call you back later. Chloe and I have some serious honeymooning to take care of."

"Honeymooning!"

A second before the phone flipped shut, Chloe heard her father's final shout.

"Just be sure you two get back to Minneapolis in time for the wedding!"

Twelve

———

They got back to Minneapolis in time for the wedding. Barely.

Mollie McGuire had it all orchestrated, rehearsed and set in motion when Mase flew them home in Chandler Industries' corporate jet. He also flew in Hannah Crockett, Harold Dobbins, bushy-bearded young Doc Johnson, retired postal worker and newest employee of Crockett General Stores, Incorporated, Charlie Thomas, and half a dozen other people he'd met only once or twice, but all of whom Chloe had invited to attend her wedding.

Throttling the engines back to a whining roar, Mase taxied the jet to his private hangar, where Emmet Fortune paced at the head of a long line of stretch limos chartered specially for the occasion. The tails of his soon-to-be father-in-law's dove gray formal coat flapped in the chill November breeze. Emmet clamped a hand on his top hat to hold it in place as the small, sleek jet rolled to a stop, then lost his headgear to a gust of wind when he rushed forward to fold Chloe into a crushing bear hug.

While father and daughter held a laughing, weeping reunion, Chloe's older brother Mac calmly went after the spinning top hat. He rescued it from the path of a rumbling fuel truck and returned to the jet to assist Mase. Courteously he directed the line of guests who climbed out to the waiting limos.

Mac's wife, Kelly Sinclair Fortune, gave her sister-in-law a ferocious hug.

"I'm so glad you're home!"

"Me, too!" The wind whipped Chloe's bangs. Scraping them back with one hand, she grinned at Kelly. "I know it's a lot to ask, even of the matron of honor, but do you think you can transform me into a proper bride during the ride to the church?"

Kelly's blue eyes twinkled. "No problem. After working all those years as your great-aunt's social secretary, I'm up to any challenge. I've got your gown, your bouquet and your hairdresser in the limo."

"Then let's get rolling."

With a wave and a promise to see Mase and Mac at the altar, Chloe ducked into the limo.

"Take Lakeshore Drive," Kelly instructed the driver. "Slowly!"

The darkened glass partition whirred up. Curling irons hissed as Jane, Chloe's hairdresser, tested them with the tip of a dampened finger. Box tops flew. Tissue paper crackled. Silk and voile and yards and yards of net swirled through the stretch limo.

By the time the silver gray behemoth pulled up at the church steps, Chloe was combed, curled, expertly made-up, gowned and veiled. A much-relieved Mollie greeted her as she climbed out of the car.

"Everyone's inside," she told the bride, her flame-bright hair shining in the sunlight. "Are you sure you want to do this?"

Chloe grinned, remembering all the times she'd stalled and put the wedding planner off.

"I'm sure."

"Well, if you're ready?"

"Mollie, wait." Chloe took her hands in a tight grip. "Mase told me about your mother and my uncle Stuart. Are you…are you all right with knowing that you're a Fortune?"

Mollie's laughter carried on the brisk November breeze. "I've known that I'm a Fortune for a long time, Chloe, and I'm more than all right with it. But if I don't get you into that church and down to the altar, your father might drum me out of the family again."

The moment she stepped through the tall wooden doors, Chloe saw that the latest addition to the family had outdone herself. Hundreds of candles gave the church's dim interior a cheerful glow. Boughs of evergreen, dotted with waxy white blooms and satin bows, decorated the pews and added a fragrant, piney scent to that of the candles.

"Mollie! Everything's gorgeous. And the pine boughs are a perfect touch."

"Mase had them flown in from the Black Hills," her newest cousin informed her as she fussed with the veil and got Emmet into position beside Chloe. "He said something about a picnic and pine needles and wanting you to remember that scent forever."

Her heart thumping, Chloe searched out the figure standing to one side of the altar.

"I will," she whispered. "I will."

A few moments later, Mollie signaled to the organist. Instantly, the music swelled into a triumphal wedding march, Kelly started down the aisle, and Emmet kissed his baby girl a final time before slowly, proudly, escorting her down the aisle.

Chloe's heart filled with joy as she smiled at the people crowding the pews. Mollie hadn't exaggerated. They were all there—her friends from Crockett, from Minneapolis, from college and high school and summer camp.

The Fortunes had all turned out, too. Every one of them. Kate, her dark red hair winged with gray, standing beside Sterling. Uncle Stuart and Aunt Marie. Her cousin Garrett, who'd disappeared with Renee Riley for a few hours at Mac's wedding and ended up marrying the beautiful deb only short weeks later. Jack and Amanda Fortune, themselves newlyweds and now full-time parents to his daughter, Lilly. Gray McGuire, Mollie's husband.

And Chad. Her twin. Her best friend. Her partner in so many youthful crimes. Chloe's smile wrapped him in love and a sincere prayer that he, too, would soon find the joy spilling through her.

Then she and her father reached the end of the aisle, and Mase stepped forward to take her hand in his. The music dimmed. The church full of people faded into the background. Eagerly, she entwined her fingers with his. With the scent of pine filling her lungs and her heart, the latest and once most reluctant of the Fortune brides pledged her love, now and forever.

Kate Fortune's eyes misted as she gazed at her radiant grand-niece. "Now that," she whispered, sliding her hand into Sterling's, "is what I call a happy ending."

"Thank goodness," he replied. "Perhaps now you can quit matchmaking and relax for a while."

The smile that had melted the staid lawyer's heart so many years ago flashed with a brilliance undimmed by age or her many adventures.

"No way! The Fortunes are as stubborn as they are loving. Sometimes they need a little help getting past the first to find the second."

Sterling swallowed a groan. He only hoped his irrepressible Kate would wait until this wedding concluded before getting to work on the next one!

*   *   *   *   *

Sometimes bringing up baby
can bring surprises —and
showers of love! For the cutest
and cuddliest heroes and
heroines, choose the Special
Edition™ book marked

That's my
baby!

SILHOUETTE
SPECIAL EDITION®

Welcome back to the drama and mystery that is the Fortune Dynasty.

A Fortune's Children Wedding is coming to you at a special price of only £3.99 and contains a money off coupon for issue one of *Fortune's Children Brides*.

With issue one priced at a special introductory offer of 99p you can get it **FREE** with your money off coupon.

Published 24 March 2000

Published 21 April 2000

Published 19 May 2000

▼™ SILHOUETTE
SPECIAL EDITION ®

AVAILABLE FROM 19TH MAY 2000

SHE'S HAVING HIS BABY Linda Randall Wisdom

That's My Baby!

Jake Roberts was everything Caitlin O'Hara wanted in her baby's father—he was fun, warm and gorgeous. They'd shared every intimate detail of their lives since childhood. Why not a baby?

A FATHER'S VOW Myrna Temte

Montana

Sam Brightwater wanted to start a traditional family. So the *last* woman he should be attracted to was Julia Stedman, who was only sampling her heritage. But Julia got under his skin and soon they were making love and making a baby…

BETH AND THE BACHELOR Susan Mallery

Beth was a suburban mother of two and her friends had set her up with a blind date—millionaire bachelor Todd Graham! He was sexy, eligible—everything a woman could want…

BUCHANAN'S PRIDE Pamela Toth

Leah Randall took in the man without a memory, but she had no idea who he was. They never planned to fall in love, not when he could be anyone…even one of her powerful Buchanan neighbours!

THE LONG WAY HOME Cheryl Reavis

Rita Warren had come home. She had things to prove. She didn't need a troublemaking soldier in her already complicated life. But 'Mac' McGraw was just impossible to ignore.

CHILD MOST WANTED Carole Halston

Susan Gulley had become a mother to her precious orphaned nephew, but she hadn't banked on falling for his handsome but hard-edged uncle. What would Jonah do when he learned the secret she'd been keeping?